The Devils We Know

A collection of short stories from New Orleans

The Devils We Know

www.grandcircuspublishing.com

Edited by Leonard Lopp

1st Edition

ISBN: 978-0-615-86868-4

Fonts provided by The League of Movable Type.
www.theleagueofmoveabletype.com/

The Devils We Know

A collection of short stories from New Orleans

Grand Circus Publishing
Detroit / New Orleans

I would like to thank all of the authors that submitted work for this inaugural release by Grand Circus Publishing. Your passion and dedication is intoxicating. Thank you for sharing your work and allowing us to share it with the world.

Thank you to the city and people of New Orleans. Your spirit and love is an inspiration to the world. You have proven time and again that your resilience and your resolve is stronger than the levees that failed to protect you.

CONTENTS

COMPANY

by Jacquelyn Milan

Lucy Dimarco wore a light-blue, sleeveless nightgown as she sat on the curved brick steps behind the house she shared with her papa. Overgrown monkey grass surrounded a narrow flagstone walkway running between the steps and an umbrella-shaped fig tree. There she stayed, a shotgun across her lap, wild red hair frizzed around her damp face and neck. In the south Louisiana town of Chalmette, with its share of short, dark-skinned Sicilians, Lucy presented an anomaly: close to six feet tall, fair skin, eyes like black crystals, and fat, very fat. When the second blue jay perched on a branch laden with figs, she raised the gun sight, blinked twice to clear her eyes, closed her left eye locking in the prey, then took aim at one of the birds pecking at a dark red fig she imagined juicy and ready to eat.

"What you doing, honey?" her papa asked, squeezing beside her bulky frame. He lowered the muzzle with his outstretched hand, voice steady and bow-shaped lips pursed.

"Those birds can't pick the best figs. Doesn't seem right. I don't have a chance." She imagined fresh figs, fig jam, and figs poached in apricot brandy, all the while wiping sweat from her face, her nose and brow wrinkled.

"Why don't you go inside and cool off? Way too hot out here. Get dressed and we'll go out for breakfast. You'd like that, wouldn't you?" her papa said.

He placed his long thin hand on her shoulder and rubbed it, his fingers massaging her tense back. She rotated her head to the movement of his hand, found his eyes, and for a moment, closed hers. The scent of Old Spice after shave lotion lingered where he touched his daughter's shoulder.

"Papa," she said, lifting the shotgun and pointing it at one of the blue jays, "I can't stand myself. Look at me. I'm getting fatter and fatter. The doctors said the meds might make me gain weight, a few pounds maybe, but nothing like this. I can't even touch my toes. There has to be something else I can do."

"It's a temporary thing," her papa called over his shoulder. He walked the path to the fig tree and shook it with both hands. The blue jays flew onto a chain link fence covered with confederate jasmine at the back of the yard, and two of the stray cats that Lucy fed, scattered. He plucked a fig and sucked the bursting red bulb, then picked a few more. The overripe bulbs he squeezed for the cats that Lucy had named Pinky and Dexter after her Chinese dry cleaners.

He turned to see Lucy staring down the barrel of the shotgun aimed at him. "Don't do that," he said, his voice flat and weary.

"Don't do what? You know, I could've had you front, back and sideways. If I shoot you, people'll just say, 'she's crazy.' I'd get away with it, too. Who cares what a crazy old woman does anyway? You always said if I ever got a notion to do something crazy, do it in St. Bernard Parish. Remember, we're connected."

He stood halfway between his daughter and the tree, about thirty feet. He stared at the barrel, then opened his mouth wide to clear his throat, or maybe to say something, she didn't know which. Then nothing moved on him. She pulled the trigger.

Nothing.

"What did you do that for? I been good to you and you treat me like this," he said, his voice hoarse, his jaw rigid. "You could give me a heart attack."

"That's all you can say?" Lucy put down the shotgun and grabbed her shoulders with her hands. Her upper body shook. "Not loaded. Don't want to take a chance hitting Pinky or Dexter."

"So what are my choices looking down the barrel of a shotgun?" her papa asked. "Sometimes I just don't get you."

Sweat rolled down her large breasts and touched her stomach. At one hundred and ninety five pounds, she easily outweighed her papa. "One of those little voices in my head told me to pull the trigger. Remember, the doctor said I'm paranoid schizophrenic. You know what that means, don't you? Simply can't trust me. A fruit cake, crazy as a loon, nuts. What are some of the other things your broads call me? It's okay, Papa, you can tell me."

"I know you wouldn't hurt your papa," he said, standing very still, the morning sun shining in his eyes. "But this isn't a game and I don't have any lady friends, not the way you mean."

"Do you like me better with the voices or like this—fat, and pushing forty?" she asked.

The voices had invaded her mind slowly at first but now they kept her company. When her mama died, a floodgate opened for the voices to rush in, even her mama's. She never lied to her daughter, the others did. The loudest ones told her to take off her clothes at the funeral home, since her mama's scent was on them. "Bury the clothes. They're Lucille's," the voices commanded.

At seventeen years old, Lucy had looked like a beauty queen, tall with flowing red hair. Undressing and climbing into the shiny cypress coffin with her mama, she was ready to obey the voices. Her papa restrained her and covered his daughter with his black suit jacket until Lucy's Aunt Sis stepped in. Someone called the Sheriff's Office, and before she knew what was happening, a deputy carted Lucy, howling like a banshee, to Charity's mental ward for a psychiatric evaluation and the first of many stays there.

"Nothing's that simple, but the pills help you," her papa said. "It takes time and that's all I've got to offer on such short notice, honey."

"You don't have a clue. I feel like shit most of the time. If it's not voices, it's the contempt for the way I look, and god, the constant nausea. Most times my thoughts run into each other. All the reading I used to do, and now I read the same sentence over and over. It's not fun, Papa."

Lucy had been a good student, but never popular. Her trademark smart mouth didn't endear her to the more conventional female classmates. The girls cringed. The boys howled and encouraged the outbursts and outrageous antics that they wished they had thought of first. She didn't wait to be asked her opinion. She gave it with the quick wit of a television evangelist delivering a sermon—clever and full of confidence.

The scarce friends she had showed up at the funeral. As time passed and word got around of her trips to the psych ward, she was alone, just her papa and family. First to leave were the not-so-close friends, then the ones she counted on, the ones she thought would remain as long as she needed them.

In time, medication and therapy helped give Lucy a sense of normalcy. To prove it, she found herself a boyfriend, John Alcus, who worked with her at a downtown New Orleans bank. Lucy, the teller, cooked spaghetti and meatballs, her mama's recipe, and baked a cherry pie when John Alcus, the senior teller, came to Sunday dinner, usually once a month. Summers they spent at the beach, winters at Saints' football games. They went steady. At twenty-three she wore his high school ring, smoked an occasional cigarette and learned to drink beer—things most girls experienced as teenagers, new for Lucy. For most of their dates, she drove her papa's new green 1965 Dodge coupe. John Alcus didn't own a car. They rounded out their weekends with movies and making out on the lakefront.

John Alcus stood taller than Lucy, with his crew cut, pasty skin and fleshy earlobes she liked to nibble. His fingernails were sometimes unkempt and Lucy fussed. She didn't love him, she was sure of that, but he was attentive and a good kisser and most of the time paid for their dates. Lucy was still a virgin. No one ever asked since it was expected that she would be until she married. And marrying John Alcus would be easy.

Everything changed when she called her boss an asshole in front of the other tellers. For that and past insubordination, he fired her on the spot in front of her bewildered boyfriend. John Alcus told her it wasn't good for his career to go steady with her after the tantrum their boss threw.

"Come on, who cares anyway, John?" she asked. "How many times did you tell me the bank was only a stopping off place until you finished up night school at Tulane?"

"I've met someone else at night school. Mama likes her," he said, picking at his nails.

"Gutless prick."

Her papa was right. It was too hot to sit on the back steps. Lucy walked inside and stood the shotgun in the hall closet where they kept the ammunition, leaving her papa alone.

The side yard was shady by the time her papa started washing the faded Dodge coupe parked on the driveway outside her window. She figured beneath the grime of the thirteen year old car with so many good memories, there was still some green paint left. When he finished, her papa put away the pail, shammy and hose, and told her he was going to do errands and invited her along.

"We can have breakfast at the cafeteria. It'll be a nice change," he said. "After that we can run some errands. We'll be home by two, three o'clock latest."

"No. Do I make myself clear? No," she answered, full lips rounded.

He looked angry, or maybe just tired. She could wear out anyone when the voices started. Ornery, one of her many shrinks called it. "Is that a medical term?" she'd asked him.

The center hallway held a second telephone in an alcove built into the wall, the long cord reaching into each of the bedrooms. She pulled the telephone into hers for privacy, closed the door and sat on a blue denim cushion along side her bed and dialed.

"Aunt Sis, come get me, quick, he's going to commit me," she said, her lips touching the mouthpiece for secrecy. "I just know he is."

"Why, it can't be more than nine or ten in the morning. What's going on? We went to the casino last night," Aunt Sis said. "Got home late so I'm a little foggy."

The ringing phone must have awakened Aunt Sis. "Foggy" was her way of saying "too much to drink." Lucy pictured her aunt answering the telephone, half-sitting, half-reclining in the double bed she shared with Uncle Junior, her bleached blond hair in pink foam rollers, her face gleaming with slathered cold cream, her body wrapped in a long nylon nightgown. Uncle Junior would be next to her in short pajama bottoms and shirtless. She thought she heard him growl.

"You know," Lucy said, "there was a girl up there in Charity Hospital named Vivian. Her husband was suing the State of Louisiana because when she was on pills, she shot her two children. So now he's suing the Central Louisiana State Hospital. She has state lawyers."

"You're not making sense and you're talking way too fast for me to keep up with you. It's too early for this conversation, sweetie."

Lucy heard the muffled exchange between Aunt Sis and Uncle Junior.

"It's okay, Junior, it's Lucy…off her meds." Lucy was sure Aunt Sis's hand covered the mouthpiece.

"Just listen," Lucy said, ignoring her aunt, breathing fast through her nose, sniffing the air. "Judge August Childs has been using the Parish and State officials and Uncle Bud and Mary Rodi, Verda Felix, Sammy Freloz and even mama's friend, Mrs. Brooks to attack us since 1966. Papa was in Mandeville Mental Hospital for more than two years. They were trying to get money out of us."

"Where are your pills? Where's your daddy? You know he never was in a mental hospital. You're alone, aren't you?"

"Papa promised he'd stay home. He's gone, probably got a broad with him."Lucy didn't wait for an answer.

"Anyway, in 1966, they gave me more than twenty-six electrical shock treatments. I had Mr. and Mrs. Joseph Lotz living on my land and Mrs. Delores living in our home at 208 4th Street. She refused to pay rent. I went to Helen McInnis in the parish for help. Hold on, Aunt Sis." She dropped the telephone, ran into the kitchen and grabbed a can of beer from the refrigerator and ran back.

"You still there, Aunt Sis?" she asked, drinking from the container, dribbling beer on the bedspread. "In 1969, Sammy, that asshole deputy, pulled my Kotex off of me and sexually molested me. Deputy Helen Badu wasn't in the isolation room like she should be. I lost my mind. They called Mrs. Connor, the correction officer, and the son-of-a-bitch took me to Jackson. She's taking me to court on April 23 at 2:00 P.M. That cow's from Belle Chasse."

"Today's July 29. April's not until next year, sugar. When was the last time you took your pills?"

"I don't know. It's been a while. They make me sick—and fat."

"I'm going to hang up right now. Uncle Junior and me are on our way to pick you up. Hurry up, Junior," Lucy heard her aunt say, "only God can help us. I'm going to give that brother of mine such a piece of my mind, so much we probably won't talk for a year. How could he let Lucy get like this?"

"Don't you hang up, not till I finish what happened, you hear me?" The phone went dead, but she didn't stop. "Anyway," she said to a line of ants marching along the floorboards, "my caseworker in Mandeville in 1973 said my father wasn't my father. The bitch. Well, you're missing the best part. I quit my job in 1972, came home and I got well. One of the uppity uptown bitches claimed that someone stole six thousand dollars of her money. What do you think? Maybe they're all in cahoots to drive me crazy." She pulled the telephone into the bathroom, squatted in front of the commode and threw up.

Lucy opened the large ornate medicine cabinet that hung from the ceiling on two brass rods. She touched the pill bottles and deodorant. Her hand lingered on a straight edge razor, the kind her barber used to trim her hair. She ran the razor's edge along her neck until it caught on her necklace. She bled. "Whoa," she said.

She wasn't ready to clean up blood from the bathroom floor in case she didn't die.

There were no curtains covering the open window, only a screen with an aluminum awning over it. She stepped into the tub and pulled the shower door. Warm water settled her nerves. Less rattled. She'd shower, wash her hair, and put on the new red sundress, the one that made her look like a beefsteak tomato. She'd wear the dress to please her papa. Did the clock on the linen shelf have the correct time? She wasn't sure. The shower calmed her. Now she wished she hadn't called Aunt Sis or said "no" to her papa. Even if Aunt Sis left her house with Uncle Junior right away, like she said, Gonzales was at least two, maybe three hours away since Aunt Sis dictated speed and route, and definitely wouldn't let Uncle Junior drive on the interstate.

If the voices stopped, she might take her pills. Taking the pills to stop the voices wasn't something she considered.

A marble and brass credenza pressed against the living room wall held three photos: a wedding picture of Lucy's smiling parents—her papa in his sailor's uniform and her mama in Grandma Rodi's wedding dress; Lucy's graduation photograph; and a family portrait with Lucy sitting on her mama's lap, laughing, her head pressed to her mama's bosom.

Lucy inherited none of her mama's delicate features. She would have been called petite, whereas Lucy was just pretty. When Grandma Rodi didn't think Lucy was around, she'd comment on how much her papa had changed from the handsome sailor in the wedding photograph. His curly black hair and dangling forelock were replaced with shiny gray and black, closely sheared waves, the chiseled cheekbones and fine nose now a gaunt, hawk-like profile.

The cool living room gave Lucy comfort as she sat there stroking the wooden stock of the shotgun just as she'd petted Pinky or Dexter when they rubbed her fat ankles to let her know they were hungry. The soap's fragrance on her skin and the texture of starch on the red sundress calmed her. She'd wait for her papa no matter how long he stayed away. He told her he would be home early, but she figured it took a long time to complete admittance papers. She'd wait.

Her mouth salivated for another drink. Two or three beers were never enough. Once she started, the light-headedness lured and cajoled her into finding comfort before complete denial. Two empty beer cans rested next to a sweaty glass, condensation rolling down the small schooner. She drank fast. She was on her way to drunkenness with an ache in the front of her head. Her shrink referred to it as her frontal lobe.

The green Dodge pulled across the ditch packed tight with oyster shells before stopping in the paved driveway. Lucy reclined in front of the picture window with a view of the street when the voices started. Her mama sat in the chair opposite the television dressed in a new floral housecoat, a Mother's Day gift, and an icepack on her forehead for her perpetual headache. She coughed night and day once the cancer had taken over her lungs, one step before death. The car door slammed and Lucy's mind raced backward, so far back that she saw her mama squeeze her papa's hand and touch the thin gold necklace around Lucy's neck. Lucy told the voices she didn't believe in God. Her life was the work of the devil.

There were other voices too: the deputy who drove her to Mandeville, the social worker who wrote the answers on the application form, and the technician who strapped her to the table at Mandeville Mental Hospital. She remembered him in particular. It was John Alcus disguised as a tall Mexican. Whoever heard of a tall Mexican? So it had to be John Alcus. She couldn't read his name because his badge was hidden in his shirt pocket, but the dirty nails were a dead give-away. He called her a Communist and she screamed, *Fascist*. Mrs. Smith, a nurse, told her they never tied her down for any psychological tests. Lucy knew better, Mrs. Smith was a damn liar.

Her papa moved across the front lawn like a man on a mission. He pulled the screen door so hard the latch popped, frightening Lucy, groggy after four beers. He wore khaki pants and a button-down blue shirt that heightened his tan skin, stretched and shiny. Lucy sat upright.

"Well, it's about time you came home," Lucy said. "Don't tell me you were out with one of your girl friends. I know what you been doing. You think I'm stupid? You're planning to admit me to Charity, aren't you? When are they coming for me?"

"Dammit," her papa said. "I put the pills in your hand. I poured the water. I set the timer for the next round of pills. I do everything but take the pills for you. You didn't take them? You're pushing me really hard. Maybe what you need is a trip to Charity and a couple rounds of shock treatment. That'll get rid of the voices for a while until you take the pills regular. But," he paused, "for your information, I stopped at the grocery for—"

The shotgun fired upward from the position on her lap. Her papa lifted his arms across his face. His movements surprised her. Did he expect the blast? She didn't. Yes, she loaded the shotgun to warn him, not shoot him. Her heart flittered like the butterflies in the backyard—faster, faster. Blood swelled in her throat as she watched the red liquid foam and effervesce from her papa's mouth. She choked. Maybe she would die, too.

He fell in slow motion. The lead pellets entered his chin and exited out the side of his ear, the right side of his face gone. She figured she pulled the trigger as it rested at an angle across her lap. The voices raged and screamed in unison, confusing her. She wasn't sure how it happened. The voices sang a litany: *Lord, have mercy. Christ, have mercy. Lord, have mercy. Ora pro nobis. Pray for us.*

Lucy swung her heavy frame off the recliner, her thighs leaving an impression on the imitation leather. Sometimes reality didn't match the voices. Today wasn't one of those days. *You killed him*, the chorus sang. Sticky blood pooled on the carpet's surface. She'd have to replace it or do something about it. After all, company was coming over.

Lucy didn't know her neighbor's first name. If she had heard it, she couldn't remember. Mama and Papa called the neighbor Brook. To Lucy she had always been kind Mrs. Brooks. There had been a Mr. Brooks, but that was a long time ago. No one talked about him. The next-door neighbor stood in the side yard. There was no doubt she'd heard the shot. What was she waiting for? Why didn't she call the Sheriff's Office? Lucy walked down the driveway to her neighbor's drive. "Mrs. Brooks, call the Sheriff. I just killed Papa."

"What are you saying? You're off your medicine again, aren't you? You hiding them around the house?"

"I know you heard the shot, now call the Sheriff's Office," Lucy said, pulling her hair off her neck, her face and dress splattered with blood. Everyone knew she was off her meds. Everyone knew her business. The voices must have told Mrs. Brooks. "I'm gonna wait in the drive for them. I guess you can tell them it's no hurry."

"Let's see if we can help," Mrs. Brooks said, moving across the two driveways. "Maybe there's no need to call the sheriff at all."

"Look at me, Mrs. Brooks. The blood. There's blood all over the living room. Papa's dead." When Mrs.

Brooks stood next to her in the driveway, Lucy opened her hand. "See—blood."

Lucy's red sundress stood in sharp contrast against Mrs. Brooks' 1950s pink brick, ranch-style house, but in the harsh sunlight, the drying blood seemed invisible on the red fabric. No wonder Mrs. Brooks seemed confused.

It took less than ten minutes for the cruiser to arrive. Lucy ran toward the deputy, her big legs moving faster than she expected. "I killed my papa. I shot and killed him. He was late so I shot him," she screamed, flapping her dress at him.

"Where's he at?" the deputy asked, walking back with Lucy to Mrs. Brooks.

"In the living room next door, where I live," she said, leaning against the house with Mrs. Brooks beside her. "My heart's burning."

"Lucy, what have you done," Mrs. Brooks said, looking towards the house and the deputy.

When the deputy returned, Lucy asked, "Is he dead?"

The young deputy covered his mouth, his face pale except for a streak of her papa's blood on his cheek and hand. He had touched him.

"Half his head's gone. Yeah, he's dead, sister. Must've went to the grocery, 'cause there's a grocery bag with ice cream in it."

"No, he was committing me. That's what took him so long." Lucy folded her body onto the grass in Mrs. Brooks' driveway. She pulled off her sandals and raised her dress over her head, displaying pink layers of fat between her panties and bra, her thick legs crossed at the ankle in the deep, cool St. Augustine grass.

"Don't worry, Mrs. Brooks, papa'll drive me to the hospital. He's a good man. He'll look after Pinky and Dexter and keep them out of the animal pound. Anyway, it's probably time for me to go. He's usually right about these things. I just can't do anything right with voices in my head. It wasn't Mama talking. It was that bitch social worker who told me my papa wasn't my papa and he was going to put me in Charity." Lucy blinked twice. The third time she kept her eyes closed, then opened them slowly.

It wasn't a dream. She turned to the deputy. "Where's the ice cream? Company's coming."

THE EMPTY THRONE

by James Nolan

The message was waiting for Wally Wiggins on his answering machine when he came home from the gym sweating like a potbellied pig. In a gruff voice choked with emotion, his father announced that Wally had just been elected this year's king of the Krewe of Mirth. At first Wally thought the voice mail was a joke or some kind of mistake, so he played it again, never imagining that it would lead to the most humiliating night of his life.

He knew, of course, that everyone in the uptown Carnival organization owed his wheeler-dealer father a favor, and wondered how many arms he had to twist to engineer this unlikely coup. Last year, after Wally's krewe membership had lapsed for quite a while, his father restored it as a fortieth birthday present, muttering that time was a-wasting and he was waiting for his only son to accomplish something that would do the family proud. In their social circles in New Orleans, that could only mean becoming an Episcopal priest, making several million dollars, marrying a debutante, or reigning as the king of a Mardi Gras parade.

"Or are you waiting to be elected queen?" his father once asked, eying his son's blousy shirt, tight denims, and maroon kid boots.

That had hurt Wally. It really did. He was a Wiggins, after all, not some queer on Bourbon Street.

His father, a ball-bearing baron and past king of Mirth himself, never stopped telling his son that "the position for my heir apparent is still open." Wally was used to his father's disappointment in him, but lately it had become his own. Maybe he really didn't try. He lived with his boyfriend, Nelson, in a drab apartment complex in Metairie, maintained the appearance of a lackluster decorating business on the Internet, and was still drinking far too much. No matter how regularly he worked out on the gym's cardio machines, he had an ample spare tire and slumped shoulders, and except when he studied himself in a full-length mirror, his father's thundering admonitions to stand up straight went unheeded.

After listening to the message for a third time, he vowed to stop boozing, but then—wait a minute—reminded himself that heavy drinking was part of the royal duties of a Carnival king. So he toweled his face, ran a pudgy hand through his spiky buzz-cut, and poured himself a double Johnny Walker Black Label on the rocks before calling Daddy.

"Sorry I missed the krewe meeting," he lied, "but I was consulting with some rich clients about their new solarium." Wally only had three steady customers, all of them penny-pinching Presbyterian bridge partners of his mother's. Without his grandparents' trust fund that Daddy doled out to him each month, he couldn't pay the rent.

"Just as well you weren't there," his father said, clearing his throat. "The vote was easier that way. Now I'm really doing this for your mother, so she can finally see you sitting up there on the throne where she raised you. And I'm only asking one thing in return."

"What?" Wally's father was a shrewd negotiator. "That I lose weight?"

"Of course not. There you go again sounding like your mother. Real men don't worry about their figures, son."

"Well then, what?"

"That if the feds are pussy enough to pass this gay marriage business, you won't marry that bum you're living with. If you did that, swear to God, I'd cut you off without a cent. And take back the Honda Accord."

Wally cast a long look a Nelson, slumped on the sofa with wet hair in front of the TV. Wet hair in the middle of the day usually meant one thing. Often when Wally went to the gym, his boyfriend slunk off to a skanky bathhouse in the French Quarter, where he engaged in God knows what acts with hustlers, tourists, and other riffraff. Nelson's sculpted pecs had sagged into tits, his hairline of springy curls was receding into a widow's peek, and his default expression had become a sullen pout, like a baby denied its bottle. True, at one time he really knew how to make Wally grab the headboard and beg for more, but lately he seemed nothing but a bad habit, like smoking or video poker.

"Don't worry, Daddy," Wally said. "That's the last thing I'd ever do."

"I couldn't bear to introduce that loser as my son-in-law to neighbors here on the North Shore or friends at the Pickwick Club."

"Good riddance to bad rubbish, if you know what I mean." Wally rattled the ice cubes in his glass.

"Congratulations, son. Your mother and I can't wait to see you on that float. It'll make our lives complete."

Wally hung up the phone, and glancing at himself in the mirror, squared his shoulders. "Hey, Nelson," he shouted like a drill sergeant, "don't you think it's time you started dinner? Tonight's your turn. And not to get into it again, but where the hell were you this afternoon?"

This was in early January, just after Twelfth Night, when in great secrecy the Carnival organizations chose their royal courts. Then the city sprang into action. With basting pins between their lips and measuring tapes around their necks, seamstresses plugged in their idle sewing machines and, in a frenzy of tulle, satin, and sequins, took measurements for the queens' and maids' ball gowns, as well as for the tunics worn by pages, dukes, and kings. Parade routes were mapped out while the viewing stands went up in front of Gallier Hall and the exclusive social clubs along St. Charles Avenue. These preparations added a certain champagne fizz to the cold, damp air, and people drank an extra cocktail before dinner because—what the hell—it was Carnival. How could they ever get through a whole winter without it?

For Wally and Nelson in their cinderblock one-bedroom overlooking the cracked, empty swimming pool, things weren't going well. At the moment, Nelson was packing his belongings into empty liquor boxes, preparing to move back in with his former roommate in the French Quarter, a skinny guy named Kirby.

"At least Kirby has a job," Wally said, downing his third scotch. "But how long do you expect him to carry you on his phone company salary? Are you two still, you know . . . ?"

"Get out of here, you jealous bitch. At least I won't have to put up with somebody snooping around in my sock drawer, looking for other guys' phone numbers."

"You yourself said—"

"No I didn't."

Wally threw his highball glass against the living room wall, where it shattered over the TV. "Damn it, I want you to stay."

Nelson folded beefy biceps over his melting pecs. "Make me."

"I need your help to get through this . . . king thing."

"Okay. But as the king's consort, can I watch the parade from the balcony of the Pickwick Club with your parents?"

Wally stared at this former supermarket clerk and wondered how he had ever considered him the love of his life. That was where he'd met him, working in the nine-items-or-less checkout line at Winn-Dixie, and for a long time his life revolved around dating Nelson. Once Nelson lost his job and moved in with him, Wally distanced himself from the Uptown world where he grew up, a snooty milieu of private schools and charity organizations in which the new boyfriend, happy with his action movies, six-packs, and pizza, stuck out like a sore thumb. Now Wally tried to picture express-line Nelson standing in a circle of bankers next to his father on the balcony of the fancy men's club. "Out of the question," he sputtered.

"So I'm supposed to watch Miss High-and-Mighty parade by from a street corner while I scrabble with drunk tourists over throws?"

A brilliant inspiration popped into Wally's mind. In any case, it seemed like a good idea at the time. He picked up the phone to dial his mother, whom he hoped could cajole the old man into honoring her son's request.

Eventually it was decided, over Mr. Wiggins dead body, that Nelson would ride on the king's float as page captain, the adult in charge of keeping in line the ten-year-old pages surrounding the throne. Wally reasoned that if he planned to drink, he'd need Nelson's help in climbing on and off the monstrous float, and besides, he wanted somehow to share this moment of glory with him. Better things were on the way for Wally, of that he was sure, but for for the moment he needed Nelson at his side.

Later that evening, after Nelson unpacked his boxes, Wally was looking forward to some great make-up sex. "Everything of yours can stay except for that pole lamp," he said, surveying the minimalist living room with a decorator's eye.

"But that was my mother's," Nelson said, "the only thing of hers I have."

Wally threw open the door. "Out with it."

"Bitch."

On the Friday afternoon of the Mirth parade, while Wally was putting the finishing touches on his regal pancake makeup, Nelson came home with wet hair. That did it. Wally hadn't eaten anything all day and his nerves couldn't take it.

"I know where you've been," Wally shouted, draining a glass of Johnny Walker rimmed with smudges of lip liner. "Start putting on your costume."

"Man, what a hunk that guy was. You should've seen—"

Wally dove for this throat.

They stumbled out of the cramped bathroom and into the bedroom, where Nelson picked up a bronze table lamp and threatened to brain Wally unless he settled down. Wally turned to face the mirror, where he smoothed out his makeup and fastened the pageboy wig in place on his throbbing head. He draped the burgundy velvet cape over his shoulders, took a nip from the pocket flask of scotch secreted in an inside pocket of his gold lamé tunic, and turned to face the miserable excuse for a man to whom he felt unbearably yoked.

"All hail His Majesty, King of Mirth," Nelson said, trying to fasten behind his back the tunic he was struggling to put on.

"Let me help you," Wally said, pulling at the stuck zipper. Then he ran his fingers through his partner's wet curls and, face frozen in a grease-paint grimace, yanked as hard as he could. "Whore," he hissed into Nelson's ear.

"Lemme go, you hysterical queen."

"King," Wally said.

"Get out of my life, you big fat. . . flop. Your old man is right about you."

"First get your sleazy ass out my house."

They were still going at each other like this at four when the black stretch limousine pulled up in front of the apartment complex to bring them to the beginning of the parade route. And they continued to pummel each other with insults and slaps like quarreling school boys, as Wally got drunker and drunker and Nelson grew more incensed. Finally the chauffeur turned up the car radio until Al Johnson's "It's Carnival Time" drowned out the two bickering royals in the back seat, their wigs askew and makeup smeared.

While the kerosene flambeaux were being lit with great ceremony at the corner of Napoleon and Tchoupitoulas, Nelson managed to shove the butt of the besotted King of

Mirth up the shaky ladder, giving him a slap on the rump as Wally staggered onto the tinseled float. The pages, already in place, looked at each other, giggling. Then the tractor-drawn float jolted into motion, and following the strutting flambeaux carriers, swayed under a canopy of oak limbs as crowds gathered to cheer the parade on its way down the darkened Uptown avenue.

With a golden scepter in one hand and the pocket flask hidden in the folds of his cape in the other, Wally gestured and waved to the throngs, gestured and waved, already impatient to reach the Pickwick Club at St. Charles and Canal. That was where he would rise from his carved gilt throne to toast his parents on the balcony, which, after all, was the point of this whole ordeal. He should have eaten something this afternoon before he started drinking, and he really needed to pee, but ancestral duty called, even as he calculated the number of major intersections the parade had to cross before getting to Canal Street. Yet he knew that his life would be different from this moment on, when he'd assume his rightful place in the world as a Wiggins.

If only he didn't need to pee so badly. Wally glanced up at Nelson standing by his side, obviously having the time of his life, and blinked, certain that he saw him naked except for a skimpy white towel wrapped around his waist. Was this what he looked like at that Quarter bathhouse? Wally couldn't shake this soused vision of his boyfriend, and startling the pink-cheeked pages, began screaming "you whore" as he gestured and waved, gestured and waved, his shouts drowned out by the high-school band ahead marching to their brassy version of "Thriller."

By the time they reached Washington Avenue, the King of Mirth was sitting with legs crossed, concentrating on his bladder. When the parade stalled a few blocks down the avenue, Wally saw it was time to act. The marching band stopped playing, then its members broke formation and milled around, high-fiving each other. The flambeaux carriers extinguished their torches and lit up cigarettes. Word soon spread along the street that the tractor of the dukes' float ahead had broken down, and that it would take a few minutes for a replacement to arrive. Tourists checked their watches and looked concerned, but most of the crowd along the curb shrugged, as if used to how things worked—or didn't work—in New Orleans.

At that moment Wally spotted the Dunkin' Donuts on the corner.

"Get the ladder and help me down off this thing," he commanded Nelson, pointing. "I'm going to use the bathroom in the donut shop."

"But it's closed," Nelson said.

True, the overhead lights were off inside and a "closed" sign hung on the door, but the tilted trays of donuts were still back-lit inside their glass display cases. Wally could swear he glimpsed a lady in a white dress moving around among them.

"The ladder," Wally insisted. Once again he saw Nelson dressed only in the bath-house towel, and spit out, "whore."

When the King of Mirth swung his legs over the edge of the papier-mâche float as if about to climb down without any help, Nelson lowered the ladder in place. Descending one unsteady step at a time, Wally made it to the street, and then staggered toward the Dunkin' Donuts, waving his scepter and straightening his crown.

He banged and banged on the locked plate-glass door, screaming, "Lemme in."

Inside, a frumpy lady in a smudged white apron was mopping the floor in the dark, her round, creased face a moon reflecting the spectral light from the lit donut cases. When she made it to the door, she mimed closed with crossed arms and a shaking head. Wally pointed to his golden crown and then steepled his fingers in prayer.

The door cracked open, and her frizzy red hair poked out. "What you want?"

"Need to use the rest room," Wally said. "Bad."

She looked him up and down, from the glittery leotards to the auburn page-boy wig. And then, as if for the first time, she seemed to notice the parade stalled along St. Charles Avenue.

"Make it snappy," she said. "I should've been home a half-hour ago."

The fluorescent overheads snapped on, flooding the donut shop with an icy glare. Wally scurried to the men's room, and the lady went back to mopping the floor, turning up the volume on her portable radio.

After a couple of thumping blues songs came on the air, banging resumed on the glass door. Mop in hand, she trudged to the front of the shop, and there stood Nelson, eyes frantic.

"Where's the guy dressed like a king?" he asked.

"Sitting on the throne, I guess," she said, pointing to the men's room.

"I've got to get him. The parade is about to take off."

Nelson raced inside, where he collided with Wally shuffling out of the bathroom. He was still wearing his crown, but the tunic was on backwards and the burgundy cape trailed along the wet tile floor behind him.

"Sit down," he said to Nelson, cross-eyed. "I need to talk to you."

"But the parade—"

"Screw the parade," Wally said, plopping down at a Formica table and resting the heavy crown on a sugar dispenser. "Hey," he called to the red-headed lady, "any of that coffee still hot."

"You look like you could use a cup, baby." She walked behind the counter and placed a paper cup under the coffee-urn spigot.

"How about one of those glazed crullers to go with it?"

"Coming right up, your royal hiney."

"The parade is about to take off," Nelson said, banging on the table, "and here you are, having breakfast?"

"Time you and me had a talk." Wally could barely hold himself up in the chair.

Nelson blanched. "You idiot—"

"You know, I was really in love with you for a long time," Wally slurred, "but you don't respect me any more, wearing that bath-house towel in my Carnival parade."

"What the fuck are you talking about?"

On the other side of the plate-glass window, the flambeaux were being relit and the marching band was falling back into formation.

"It's time for us to call it quits," Wally said, taking a long slurp of his coffee. "You've broken my heart."

The band blasted into a full-throttled marching version of "When You're Smiling" as the crowd roared back to life. Nelson tugged at the king's tunic, but Wally wouldn't budge. Then the royal consort made a dash for the door, swung it open, and Wally's mournful brown eyes followed his back as he scampered up the ladder, dragging it onto the float behind him.

Then float by dazzling float, the parade continued to pass along St. Charles Avenue. For a moment an enormous white swan hovered under the oak branches, ridden like a bronco by a busty papier-mâche Leda with yellow foil tresses. Then other illustrations of the krewe's "Greek Shenanigans" theme rolled by, reflected in the glass window of the donut shop where Wally sat saucer-eyed, gazing out. And in the distance, the empty throne on the king's float rounded Lee Circle and then disappeared down the avenue.

For a long while, Wally said nothing, slumped over his coffee and cruller at a table in the Dunkin' Donuts, as the parade that he had waited for his whole life rolled by outside. The muffled cheers from the crowd along the route faded into the insistent buzz inside his head. He figured that by now, the king's float must have stopped in front of Gallier Hall, where he should have been toasting the mayor. And ten minutes later it should be passing under the eyes of his parents standing on the balcony of the Pickwick Club. He replaced the crown on top of his wig as fat dirty tears oozed down his cheeks, blotching the makeup and pooling on the tabletop in tan puddles.

"Trouble back home at the castle?" the donut lady asked, eyebrows raised.

"What's your name, sweetheart?"

"Evelyn," she said.

"I don't know what . . ." Wally blew his nose with a honk.

"That's okay, baby," she said, coming around to join him at the table. "It's not much better at my house. My husband left me this week, after twelve years. Mind if I sit down?"

"Why'd he do that?"

"Split with a younger woman," she said, taking a seat, "some dame he met Cajun dancing at Rock n' Bowl while I was here working the night shift."

"That's not fair."

"Like they say about love and war. What's your story?"

"My daddy has always run roughshod over my momma," Wally said, "but in some ways they have the perfect marriage. And I always thought one day I'd have something rock solid like that, but you saw what I'm stuck with."

"He's not so bad, considering what's out there."

"Plays around on me. To my face."

"Maybe it's time to trade him in." Evelyn shot him a wicked grin.

"The stupid part is," Wally said, wiping his eyes with the velvet cape, "not being with him would be like cutting off my leg. I really love that damn man."

"I can tell you do. And I adore my husband," she said, shaking her head, "but I ain't taking him back when he gets tired of two-stepping."

"And what will Daddy and Momma say now that I've screwed up this?" He rapped his scepter on the table, knocking over the sugar dispenser. "I couldn't even sit on a throne with a crown on my head. That's all they asked of me."

"Well, Your Majesty, some jobs are tough, and this one better be here tomorrow," Evelyn said, rising from the table and reaching for the light switch, "or my two kids will starve." The overheads went out.

The opening organ chords of Toussaint McCall's "Nothing Takes the Place of You" were swelling from the radio as Evelyn returned her mop and sloshing bucket to the broom closet. Wally hoisted himself to his feet, wondering what he was going to do now. Nelson was the steady hand that anchored him, the only person who could calm him down and lead him home. Where was he?

"Want to dance?" he asked.

"With you?" Evelyn asked, eyes widening.

"Why not? It's Carnival."

He wrapped an arm around her waist, and she snuggled close to him.

"Don't be getting any ideas," he said.

"Oh honey, you're just like my sissy brother. I know you go to another church."

"Why, what you got against Episcopalians?"

While the red lights of a crash truck flashed outside, announcing the tail end of the Krewe of Mirth, Wally and Evelyn slow-danced to the smoldering torch song along the slippery floor in front of the illuminated donut cases, watery eyes closed tight as if dancing alone with lost dreams.

I moved your picture
from my walls
and I replaced them
both large and small.
And each new day
finds me so blue
because nothing, oh nothing
takes the place of you.

"You are my queen . . . ," he murmured.

"And you my king . . . ."

"For a day. . . ."

"Or tonight," said the donut lady, pulling him closer.

Wally didn't know he could walk so fast. Maybe it was the coffee or a sugar rush from the cruller or the sweet kiss Evelyn planted on his cheek as he left the Dunkin' Donuts, but now he bounced along Tchoupitoulas Street, steadying the crown on his head while the velvet cape ballooned behind him with wintry gusts of fog blowing in from the river. He simply had to make it to Poydras Street, where the parade would be disbanding, to catch the limo waiting there to take him home. He'd left his cell and wallet in the car, and now with no money, ID, or credit cards, he could foresee an even more demeaning night ahead, with the King of Mirth wandering up and down Canal Street trying to cage cab fare from tourists.

The first thing he spotted was the enormous flying goose or swan or whatever in the hell it was, looming over a stalled float on the other side of the intersection. By now most of the riders must have already dispersed to the krewe's after-party at the Sheraton, where in his present circumstances Wally wouldn't have been caught dead. He couldn't imagine the hubbub that the empty throne probably caused when the king's float pulled up in front of the mayor's viewing stand or under the balcony of the Pickwick Club, where his parents would have been waiting.

His head hung so low that the crown tumbled off. He picked it up and kept on walking, wondering if Nelson would go with him to live in Atlanta or Houston, wherever Wally didn't have to live up to anything. His life was over in this town, where he'd never be his daddy's son.

Just as he was crossing Poydras, a limo cut him off and then screeched to a halt. The back window slid down as Nelson's widow's peak emerged. When their glances locked, they both froze, staring at each other for a long while.

Nelson's slate eyes softened as his face turned tender, and whether the expression conveyed love, understanding or only pity, Wally fell into it as though coming home. Nelson swung open the limo door and scooted over. While climbing inside, Wally's pocket flask slipped from his tunic pocket and clanked into the gutter, which was right where he left it.

He inched closer to Nelson, fidgeting with the crown and cape and scepter, not daring to speak. Nelson reached for his fingers and they sat there, hand-in-hand, not saying a word as the limo plowed through the honking post-parade traffic on Poydras.

Wally's cell phone lit up, vibrating on the tray table next to him.

He recognized the number. Daddy.

"It's the queen mum," his mother's voice said, breathless, "and Wally, we're so sorry. Will you ever forgive us? The Causeway was fogged in tonight, so we had to take the long way into town from the North Shore, through Slidell. We've just left our car in the parking garage next to the club, but missed the whole parade. We're devastated that we didn't see you on that king's float. I told your father we should have left by four, what with the Carnival traffic, but listen to me making excuses. I'm sure other members took loads of pictures. How was your ride?"

"Fine," Wally muttered.

"We're so proud of you. Look, let me give you to your father. He's bursting, I tell you, just bursting."

Wally winced. "Okay."

His father's booming voice seemed to fill the entire limousine. "So, son, how did it feel to toast the mayor of New Orleans from the king's throne of Mirth?"

Wally calculated how long it would take, once his parents made it into the Pickwick Club, for word to reach them that the throne on the king's float was empty as it passed under the balcony tonight.

Maybe five, ten minutes at most.

"Daddy, thanks so much for everything," Wally said. "I've never been so happy and proud as I was waving up there on that throne."

They were still his, these five or ten minutes he had left as his father's son, all he'd ever have.

And he knew that now they would have to last him a lifetime.

THE MOON CAME UP WRONG

by P. Curran

What happened to Joe Ianno was, they removed a tumor from the back of his head and while recovering at home he went crazy. Suddenly just before sunrise he came stumbling down Rampart, naked, shouting at strangers. I saw him from inside Katy's, so I went out to help him. Joe had no idea who I was. He died in the back of a cop car going to the hospital. So maybe that primed me for the Polly thing the next morning.

I was drinking in Checkpoint's and I'd told the story about Joe Ianno fifteen or twenty times during the course of the night. Dull gray light began creeping in the windows. I went to take a piss.

When I came out Jack the bartender said, "Do me a favor?"

"Sure," I said.

"I can't leave here," Jack told me. His cheeks had gone slack and his brows had knit. "Would you please go help them?

"Help who?"

"Just go down Esplanade this way," Jack said, pointing with his thumb. "The girl with the long brown hair. She has another girl with her. Just go help them look for her dog?"

"Okay," I said.

"Some guy jumped her, and her dog ran away," Jack explained.

I went. Nothing I'd call sunshine lit the clouds or the roofs yet, but by the time I caught up with the two girls, the sky had lightened considerably from when I'd stepped out of the bar. The shift between night and day gave my vision a weird vibrancy. Soft purple shadows outlined every contour of the trees and the buildings and the two girls.

I recognized one of them right away, though I never remember her name. She's tall with short hair and has Betty Page tattooed on her left arm. She tends bar but changes jobs too often for me to remember where.

Then the girl with the brown hair turned around, and it was Polly. I happen to know Polly doesn't like me.

(I first met Polly a few minutes before the start of her first day in New Orleans, four or five years ago. I used to talk to strangers a lot more then. Plus, she's so beautiful. She had arrived by bus around midnight. I met her at maybe four-thirty, in the front window at Molly's on Decatur. Her name was short for Polymnia, a street uptown. She said her father, who had grown up in New Orleans, gave her the name. For a few minutes I made Polly laugh. Out of the blue I began to make fun of a bum outside the bar, an older street crazy wearing a stovepipe hat and listening to a transistor radio. He'd been on Decatur since I moved to town, so I could mimic him pretty well. I didn't know he was Polly's father.)

Polly spun around to glare at me, and her eyes were puffy from crying. I put my hands up and asked, "What kind of dog are we looking for?"

Looking away, Polly slid her right hand back and forth horizontally at thigh level. "He's this big," she said, "white with a brown patch around his eye."

Her friend said, "Here come the cops."

I walked away from them onto the side street. Royal, I think it was. I went to Kerlerec and turned right. No sign of the dog. Halfway up the block I noticed dogs sleeping in two different yards, and it occurred to me that wherever Polly's dog had run to, other dogs would bark at it.

I held still and listened to the Marigny around me: cars, birds... a television in some house nearby...

I didn't hear dogs anywhere.

One policeman watched me walk back towards them. As I drew closer he seemed to find me suspicious. All three of the cops stared at me when I reached them. Immediately I told Polly, "I'm sorry, he's not over there. The dogs would be barking."

"What?" she said, angrily.

"If your dog went this way down any of those streets, the other dogs would get up and bark at him," I said. "All the dogs over there are just sleeping."

"I don't care," she said. "The little piece of shit didn't protect me, anyway. He fucking runs away."

She began saying something to the cops, but I didn't listen. I looked Polly's friend in the eye and said, "Should we go look that way?" I pointed across Esplanade.

She nodded and crossed the street with me. On the other side she said in a low voice, "I think we should just disappear."

"What?"

"We should just take off," Polly's friend said.

In silence we started down the block into the Quarter.

"Those cops are pissed," she said at last.

"At who?" I asked. "At Polly?"

She nodded. "They think she's lying. They think she made it up."

"Why would she?"

"I don't know," Polly's friend said, "but I think they're right."

Still we saw no sun, though the sky had turned pale. On the next block ahead of us, a shower of feathers washed across a speeding taxi. The car turned quickly around a corner, leaving a crippled pigeon behind to writhe on the asphalt.

"Polly's crazy, I don't know if you know her," Polly's friend explained. "She starts making things bad for herself. The cops already know she's nuts, so they'll just tell her to go home."

We turned up Barracks Street, and she added, "Besides which, I got a bag of coke in my pocket, I don't need them searching me."

"This is kind of weird," I said.

"You don't know Polly."

"No, I mean this morning," I said. "It just seems really weird. It's not dark anymore but it's still not daytime."

She sighed as we walked, and I assumed at first that she found what I'd said foolish. Then she said, quietly, "I'm not surprised. It was a weird night. The moon came up wrong."

We continued walking. Polly's dog could have trotted right past us, we would not have noticed.

"Before work last night," Polly's friend said, "I was waiting on my porch for my ride. It was dark already. I looked that way—" She pointed west. "The moon was orange, and only a half-moon. But it was the wrong half. It was the upper half. I noticed it, and then I watched and the moon became full in front of me. There must have been thick clouds covering the bottom just when I looked at it."

A cab with at least two pigeon feathers jutting from its grille came toward us on Barracks. Polly's friend hailed it. She held the door open for me and asked, "You need a ride somewhere?"

"You get in," I said, and then climbed in beside her.

She told the driver to go straight. As we crossed the intersection we peeked together down the street toward Esplanade and saw Polly wringing her hands at the police. "No, thanks," Polly's friend said.

I had her drop me at my house. When I invited her inside she laughed and said, "Sorry, I don't have enough. Have a good night."

It bothered me a little that she thought I wanted to mooch her coke. If I wanted to do coke, I could get my own easily enough. All I had wanted was to get her in bed. Cocaine users take things the wrong way, though. The drug changes the way their brain chemistry works, or something.

By this point I felt so tired that I lay down on my bed with my clothes still on. I decided that the sun would come out while I slept. Thus far, it always had.

HAPPY HOLIDAYS, JUKEY BOY

by
Joe Barbara

A man's voice was leaving a message inside on my machine as I fished the keys out of my pocket. I was on the stoop of the shotgun house, my stuff from work set on the sidewalk behind me.

"...Happy Holidays to you and yours, man," Click.

I missed the first part, but if I'd heard that last part right, whoever left the message obviously had no clue about what had been going on in my life. Wiggling the key in the lock like the landlady showed me, I decided I'd wait to see who the caller was after I caught my breath and got settled. I'd had to park a block away, lugging the laptop, a grocery bag and a bunch of books stuffed into my dark brown briefcase, a gift from Christmas past. Some people said the briefcase made me look more like a businessman than a professor, but my ex had given it to me years ago, and I guess I had kept using it just to keep the peace.

Parking in my new neighborhood, I was finding out, could be the pits when you had things to carry. Overall, though, I was satisfied with where I'd landed, in the Faubourg Marigny, one of the colorful neighborhoods of New Orleans, just downriver from the French Quarter.

On a street lined with shotgun houses, what I especially liked about the shotgun I'd decided to rent, besides the Steamboat Gothic gingerbread trim, was the working fireplace, somewhat of a rarity in the New Orleans climate. Tonight it would actually be cold enough to light it, which I planned to do while I had the chance. It would start turning muggy tomorrow, according to the weather report on the drive home, and by Christmas Eve they said it might be warm enough to run the air conditioning. Such was life in the Big Easy. But at last I was on semester break, seasonal weather or not.

As acting head of the music department, I had worked well beyond the end of the fall semester. Christmas was rushing upon me, and I still had not done a lick of shopping. I was beginning to wonder if I were already "going native," giving in to a second bachelorhood of unmade beds and dirty dishes. Leaving important shopping undone until the last minute, not to mention the shipping involved this time – that wasn't like me, or at least it hadn't been.

Though I wasn't feeling the Christmas spirit, when I stepped through the door my place smelled like a forest of Christmas trees, thanks to the gift of a potpourri the university chancellor had given me yesterday. The piney scent was an improvement over the smell of new paint I'd been greeted with since moving in.

I stooped to retrieve the day's mail off the floor and was relieved to see that Buddy, my little rescue mutt, hadn't peed on it.

The mail turned out to be a single holiday greetings card, from my new bank. Depicting nothing more than a poinsettia against a backdrop of snow, the card had the look of something that had been designed by the bank's diversity committee and run past legal to ensure it was bland enough to offend no one in the Western hemisphere. It went sailing straight into the wastebasket. I was not doing cards anymore, not this year, not this lifetime.

I hadn't always been such a Scrooge. But this would be my first Christmas since the divorce. My ex and the two boys lived out of state now, something I tried not to dwell on.

I went to the kitchen at the far end of the house and mixed a stiff Black Russian. Its sweet burn going down and the instant glow I felt were just what I needed. I was ready now to check that message and light the fireplace. After that, I'd plop down on the couch and begin what was going to be a delicious reading holiday. It would soon be dark – perfect for getting lost in the first book on my stack, a biography of Mississippi John Hurt.

I pressed the play button and leaned down to listen.

"Hey, Jukey Boy, how you and your family been, man? It's me, Mike. I can't believe I found your number from directory assistance. Listen, give me a call. I'm at the same number I always been at. Or just come by if you want. I don't go nowhere. I need to talk to you. Okay? Call me, hear…Happy Holidays to you and yours, man."

The voice was deeper and a bit gravelly, but it was Mike, all right.

It felt strange to hear Mike's voice, and stranger still to hear my old nickname. Nobody had called me "Jukey Boy" in over three decades, close to four. "Jukey Boy" came from the old-fashioned juke box I used to keep in my room when I lived with my parents. The juke box came from my grandfather, a two-fisted Irish-Italian, who had once owned a "colored" barroom, as they used to call it. The bar had been in the Shrewsbury section of old Jefferson Parish. Grandpa knew how much I liked music, and he made sure I got the barroom's jukebox after the place went out of business. The jukebox was about the size of a refrigerator and smelled of cigarette smoke and spilled drinks. But the records that came with that jukebox – blues, the real blues, were cool beyond belief. Grandpa had rigged it so that I could use the same nickel to play all the records on it as much as I wanted, and that nickel's worth of music changed my life.

Mike, my best friend from around the corner, also loved music and he too became transfixed by the raw sounds of the blues from those scratchy records. By the time we were in high school, I'd taken up guitar, and Mike had found a second-hand drum set. We started trying to replicate the sounds coming out of that jukebox. While so many wanna-be musicians our age learned the blues second-hand from British bands like Led Zeppelin and Cream, Mike and I were plugged in to the source.

Mike's dad, Mr. Erin, used to get drunk a lot and beat him raw for the tiniest infraction, so Mike stayed at our house as often as he could. Drinking must have run in Mike's family because Mike started sneaking a small ice chest full of beer with him whenever he came over to play music out in our garage. The ice chest might as well have been an extension of his body. It was always within reach, right next to his drum stool. As the Sixties turned into the Seventies and our musician friends began going behind the levee to smoke joints, Mike never joined us but would wait in my garage, drinking beers from his ice chest.

We were different in other ways, too. I was shy, wore Buddy Holly glasses and had hardly been kissed back then, while Mike was handsome as all get-out, with chiseled features, blues eyes, and an animal magnetism that had girls, and later women, throwing themselves at him. But the blues was our common ground, and we both kept getting better on our instruments. By our senior year, we both knew college was out of the question. Soon as we graduated from high school we planned to play music full-time, and that's just what we did. In our minds, that old barroom jukebox had been our real school, and Mike and I could hold our own with anybody.

We found a blues band on Bourbon Street in the French Quarter that needed a drummer and a guitar player, and before you knew it we were working six nights a week. It was grueling, but we developed some killer chops. One of my proudest moments was the time I saw Muddy Waters himself, standing on the sidewalk outside the club, bobbing to the groove we were putting down.

That gig lasted two years, until the club owner got rid of the band and hired a DJ to play disco. Suddenly desperate for money, Mike started playing with a cover band grinding out Top 40 hits. I managed to scrounge up a four-string banjo, tune it like a guitar, and started playing traditional New Orleans jazz, although most everybody still called it Dixieland back then. And just like that, we drifted apart.

Looking back with a clearer head, those years of playing on Bourbon Street were actually some of the lowest times of my life. Just as Mike never stopped reaching into that ice chest, I never stopped rolling joints. I lived in a fog both metaphorically and literally. A couple of incidents back then were the lowest of the low. I used to talk to Alicia, a waitress at the club, during the breaks. She was sweet and I thought she seemed out of place working on Bourbon Street. I fantasized about running off with her and getting married. Slowly, I was working up the courage to ask her out. Too slowly, as it turned out, as she died tragically before I made my move.

Apparently Alicia had too much to drink on one of her off nights, went out walking and was crushed by a train out in Kenner where she lived, near the airport. Her body was mangled almost beyond recognition, they said. Other than old people, Alicia was the first person I ever knew to die. That someone so beautiful and full of life could be gone from this world forever rattled the hell out of me. I had nightmares and was spooked by the dark for a long time after that. Mike, too, seemed extremely flipped out by what had happened, and refused to talk about it.

Then there was a near-tragedy that rattled me even further. Sometime close to the end of our run on Bourbon Street, Mike and I and some friends were at the Lake Pontchartrain seawall partying one night. I was drinking, stoned and showing off in front of some women. I dove off the concrete seawall into the dark waters of the lake and swam some distance from the shore. The water was colder than I was expecting and when I turned around to swim back I started cramping and couldn't stay afloat. I swallowed a mouthful of water while I was slipping below the surface and in a panic realized this is how my life would end, by drowning.

Mike, even as loaded as he had to have been, sensed something was wrong. He dove in, swam out to where I was, grabbed me, and got me back to the bottom step of the seawall. I puked my guts out and lay there unable to move for what seemed like an eternity.

From that night, I regarded Mike as someone to whom I would always be indebted for grabbing me from the jaws of death in the nick of time. Even when we no longer regularly kept in touch, I continued to feel that way. My brush with death also precipitated a self-assessment of where my life was going. I quit hashish and weed, cut back on drinking, and decided to go to a local college and study music. I took to academia pretty well and carved out a niche as a blues and jazz scholar, finding a way to hang on to the music I loved. When I got a job teaching in the music department as a grad student, I quit the night life and never looked back.

I was haunted by Mike's message all that night and into the next day. Making a halfhearted attempt at some late afternoon Christmas shopping, I was unable to concentrate, wondering why he called. Part of me dreaded revisiting anyone or anything I associated with such a dark time in my life. Still, the sense of lifelong indebtedness made not responding to Mike out of the question. In the midst of hordes of shoppers in the mall, I called it a day, even though I was still empty handed. I needed to go see Mike.

On the drive over to Mike's I decided to stop first for some coffee and to peruse the latest issue of *Rolling Stone* I had in the car. About the only reason I subscribed to that rag anymore was to check its obituaries to see if I recognized any artists and music biz people from the Sixties and Seventies who had gone on to that big jam session in the sky. Now that we were almost a decade into the next century, it was a rare issue that didn't have somebody I used to listen to in the obits.

I flipped through the pages of the magazine and sipped a cup of Sumatra strong enough to rattle my fillings. It would soon have me sweating because the mugginess the weatherman had talked about was arriving. It seemed more suitable outside for a barbeque than for caroling, yet the coffee shop's windows were stenciled with fake snow, and the sound system was cranking out wintery holiday ditties by Sinatra, Crosby, Mel Torme, Nat King Cole, Elvis and Burl Ives.

Was this place *trying* to depress people? Hello?

This was New Orleans, the sub Tropics, people. We didn't roast chestnuts on open fires. It was too damn hot for that. We didn't make happy, jolly snowmen down here. If we did the snowmen would probably get shot at in a drive-by. And what did all these singers whose voices were oozing out of the speakers in the ceiling have in common? They were all goddamn dead.

The way I was feeling I was ready to just skip the Christmas holidays and fast forward to Mardi Gras.

Thank God, by the time I was getting ready to leave they played Anne Murray's rendition of "Winter Wonderland." It was not that I was an Anne Murray fan, but finally we had a song by a singer who was not lying in a cemetery somewhere.

I was trying to be positive. I really was. I just wasn't succeeding.

It was around dusk when I turned off of Jefferson Highway onto Mike's old street in the sleepy old neighborhood I had bicycled and walked through thousands of times in my youth. Mike had never moved out of his parents' home. After his father was killed at work in an oil rig accident, Mike's mother let him convert the shed in the back yard into a bedroom.

I flipped off the car's AC so my glasses wouldn't fog when I got out. As I passed the familiar houses, I wondered what had become of some of the parents of my childhood friends. I doubted if many of them were still around. Several of the houses marked the season with new-fangled inflatable reindeer and snowmen and motorized Santas waving at the cars going by.

I parked on the curb in front of the old wooden frame house I had known so well. Mike's house was dark – there was not even a porch light. The grass looked like it hadn't been cut since before Halloween. The concrete Virgin Mary out front, once the centerpiece of his mom's garden, was still there, now surrounded by weeds and tilting like the Tower of Pisa. It occurred to me as a I walked up to Mike's house that I should have brought something, a tin of cookies or something. Too late for that now.

Judging from the peeling paint and missing shutters it was a safe bet the doorbell didn't work, so I knocked. A shrunken woman in a faded, loose-fitting dress answered the door. Mike's mom.

"Hey, Miss Maureen, so good to see you. Merry Christmas." From the hug I gave her I wasn't sure if her weight made it into triple digits.

"Merry Christmas," she said, smiling. "Did you bring the sausage?" she added, her face continuing to beam what seemed to be delight at seeing me. I could tell she had no clue who I was.

"No, Miss Maureen, I just came by to see Mike. It's me. Steve. Jukey Boy." She kept smiling, saying nothing. She stepped aside to let me in.

I heard a toilet flush. Then the house started rattling with each heavy footstep coming down the hall. A sound of labored breathing replaced the awkward silence between Miss Maureen and me.

"Hey, what it is, Jukey Boy..." That was a far as Mike got before he started hacking, and possibly aspirating, from the sound of it. His coughing fit was so intense that I was wondering, as he turned colors, whether I'd be doing CPR before the visit was over.

"I'm all right," he rasped, huffing, raising up a thick hand to assure me. "I'm like this all the time."

There was enough semblance to the man I remembered to know it was Mike, but I was speechless at what I was seeing. Looking at him in the dim light, it was as if the head of a gargoyle had been placed on the body of a Sumo wrestler. His face was splotched with broken blood vessels and he had tripled in size, easily.

Mike offered a sweaty hand, which I shook, grateful he didn't want to give me hug. Stale body odor filled the room as he stood there shirtless.

"Let's have some cookies, man," Mike said. "Hey, Ma, bring me a tee shirt," he yelled.

I followed Mike to the kitchen at a funereal pace, him huffing the whole time. Miss Maureen was known for baking some of the best cookies around, and I wondered if she still had the touch, but when we got to the kitchen, Mike tore open package of store-brand vanilla wafers.

"Here," he said, tilting the bag toward me. "Mr. Johnny next door gave us these 'cause I helped him change a light bulb. They pretty good. He gets them at Wal Mart over there by the Huey P. Long Bridge." Mike grabbed a couple of cookies and lit a cigarette. Miss Maureen came in and handed Mike a fresh tee shirt. "Let's go to my room," Mike said.

We went out the back door and walked across the tiny backyard to the shed. I noticed Mike had hung on carefully to the railing next to the three steps leading from the back door to the grass.

Mike's room was not that different from the way it was the last time I saw it, but it sure smelled a lot worse, like a thrift store, only stronger. I counted three ashtrays, each brimming with butts, and empty beer cans everywhere.

"I'm a sick man," Mike said. He sat on the side of his bed, trying to catch his breath. I sat in the old easy chair I remembered, the one that had been his dad's. It now had several burn marks and a tear on one of the arms with the white cotton stuffing sticking out.

"What do you, have?" I asked not sure what to say.

"Ha. What don't I have? I'll spare you the litany. Remember them altar boy words? Let's just say my heart and liver are on that lit'ny. My joints and inflammation, too." Mike started hacking again and spit into an old Styrofoam cup.

So it wasn't my imagination, the yellowish tinge to his skin I thought I detected in the dim light. That explained the filmy eyes. Mike reached over to a mini refrigerator next to his bed and popped open a 24-oz can of beer.

"You want one?" he asked, holding the refrigerator door open.

"Sure," I said, a bit uneasy about sharing the very thing that was lubricating his slide into the next world. But at this point, I figured, what the hell, the damage was done. Whatever pleasures Mike could still wrest from the land of the living, he might as well enjoy them.

"They wanted to get me hospice, but I told them I don't want none of that shit. I told them bastards, don't bring me no oxygen. Don't bring me no holy water either, unless it's got a olive in it. Ha. I'm gonna croak on *my* terms, dig? But look, Jukey Boy, I gotta tell you something. It's been eating me, man."

"Just call me Steve," I said. "Nobody calls me Jukey Boy anymore."

"Yeah, it's been a while, huh? I tell ya, chief, I'm nervous right now. I gotta tell you something. Seeing you after all these years. Shit...I'm just gonna lay it on you straight. Remember Alicia, man?" Before he could continue Mike launched into another paroxysm of coughing.

This gave me a few seconds to wonder what in the world Alicia, the waitress from the club on Bourbon Street where we used to play, had to do with anything. Even though I had no clue about her relevance decades after her death I could feel myself tensing up. Why would Mike want to bring her up, saying he needed to "lay it on me straight?"

"Of course I remember her," I said, once Mike stopped coughing. "I remember how bummed we were when she got hit by that train. I remember how you walked away whenever anybody brought her up."

"It wasn't no accident, man," Mike said, looking down at the floor, "that thing with the train...I was banging her on the side. I know you was sweet on her and everything, and she used to tell me she always thought of you as a gentleman…but I was banging her, man. I'm sorry. So, she tells me one night she was carrying my kid. Man, I did a flip out when I heard that. We started fighting. We were both drunk as shit. I beat the living shit out of her. Then I freaked, 'cause she wasn't breathing no more. I started screaming, 'Come on, baby. Come on, baby, don't do this to me.' But she already bought the farm, man. I sobered up real quick after that, like in a instant. I did what I thought I had to do. I didn't like being so cold about it, but she was dead by that point and there was nothing I could do about it. You dig? It wouldn't make no shit to her anymore what happened. She wouldn't feel nothing. Man, the thought of going to prison…no fucking way. So I threw her over my shoulder and carried her out to the railroad tracks, which was pretty close by and laid her down. I was scared shitless that somebody was gonna see me. I wanted it to look like she passed out, or maybe like she wanted to off herself on purpose."

"Jesus, Mike," I said, hyperventilating. The hair on the back of my neck was standing straight up. I couldn't look at him, this man who had once risked his life to save me from drowning.

"You gotta understand, man, I was looking out for my own ass by that point," Mike said. "Even still, I figured, I was gonna get popped one day. But I never did. For years and years I kept waiting for Sheriff Harry fuckin' Lee to show up at my door, but he never did. Nobody did. I got away with fucking murder, bra. Can you believe that shit?"

I just sat there not knowing what to say, a sharp burning sensation suddenly eating away at the pit of my stomach. Mike threw his empty beer can at a waste basket, missing it widely. He got out two more beers. Handing me one, he said, "It don't matter no more if the word's out about this. Hell, they'd be doing me a favor if they fried my ass now. But I'm gonna beat they ass to it. I got enough medicine stashed away to kill everybody on this block. I get tired of hanging on, man. It's almost hasta la vista time, baby. But I had to get this off my chest before I take my dirt nap." Looking directly at me, Mike said, "You was always somebody I could talk to."

"That's not what my ex used to say," I said, not sure if a wisecrack was appropriate.

"Your ex? Aw, don't tell me. You and your old lady split?"

"We did, but that seems so inconsequential right now."

"Whoa. Don't lay no fifty cent words on me, man. Look, I got one more thing to take care of."

Mike handed me a folded sheet of loose leaf paper that had been lying on his bed.

"Everything I told you, it's on that paper. It's all written down for prosperity. Get it? Remember how we used to joke around with words like that on stage? Man, those were some good times, huh?"

"Yeah," I said. Those times were anything but good times but I didn't want to dignify Mike's presence with any further conversation. I set my beer on the floor. I needed to leave. If I didn't owe this guy my life, I would have already been out the door.

"Maybe Alicia's folks would feel better knowing she didn't off herself or was sleeping on the tracks because she was so drunk,' Mike said as I stood up to leave. "You could probably find them better than I could, but I'll leave it up to you...are you leaving already? Ain't you gonna tell me what up with you?"

"Mike, I got some serious Christmas shopping to do," I said as he handed me the piece of paper and I like a fool took it. I was no longer thinking clearly.

"You pissed?" Mike said. "Hey, I don't blame you... some heavy shit, I know, but I feel better already, now that I told you."

I left without saying another word or shaking Mike's hand.

When I got home I picked up Buddy and held him tight, just to feel close to his innocence. I had driven home in a daze after the bombshell Mike had laid on me. One thing I decided – there was no way in hell would I try to contact Alicia's family. I remembered that her last name had been McNair and she was from Peoria. That may have been enough to track them down, but her parents might have been dead or senile by now. No. I wasn't going to look for them, and I wasn't going to call the cops. Mike had looked like he might not make it to the end of the year. I was going to let sleeping dogs lie.

I set Buddy down and unfolded the piece of paper Mike had given me. Looking it over, it was pretty much the same as what he had just told me. It felt creepy just to be holding it.

It was too warm to light the fireplace. So I just set the sheet of loose leaf on top of a partially burned log. I took the lighter from the mantelpiece and lit a corner of the page. I watched it turn black, crinkling, and twisting this way and that, reminding me of the death throes of a an old black and white movie monster. I kept watching until nothing remained but ashes.

Excerpt from
THE NAZI & THE RABBIT
by R.A.W.

The Tortured Tail of Bloodied Bum Suk Lee and Me

My life as a two-year old innocent seems like a strange dream, images I can conjure but no longer feel, as if they happened to someone else, stories I read in a book and chose to make my own.

But they *were* real.

I *was* happy.

I was a proud rabbit, strong and handsome, the envy of the Briar.

Now I'm sorta fucked, sorta lost my soul when I tossed my lot into this toss-off town at the ass-end of the Mississippi River.

I'm a can of fucking Spam in a fallout shelter.

And now look at me.

Some days, on the bad days, the real bad days, even I have a hard time accepting that I'm a rabbit.

Fuck man, look at me!

I'm living in some flooded and abandoned house in the pits of hell, post-hurricane New Orleans, hiding from crackheads and bums as they make with the flame and rock-sizzle, shedding clothes in piles of rot and refuse, fucking in mad coke-spasms, gettin' it on with crackling bone-on-bone copulation.

I have no skin. You can see that, right?

Things have gone bad in my life. That's obvious. And it's a long story that I will do my best to tell. One minute I'm hopping through the fields of paradise, and the next I'm here, in this pit of squalor, sucking on a sewage pipe for sustenance, hiding my hideous shame from the world.

It's been a downward spiral.

Here's how it went down.

The Briar excommunicated me after the disease took hold.

"No need for the likes of you 'round here," they told me.

Weed out the weak.

Even my poppa, my holy father, he sent me on my way with vengeful eyes and latent hatred.

Things went sideways.

I try to block out the memories but it's all I can think of.

It consumes me.

Have you ever been attacked by a memory over and fucking over again? I'd call up an exorcist but this new life of mine has no room for religion or hope. It's all about acceptance and running out the clock.

I knew something was wrong when I emerged from behind the redberry bush after my romp with Honda Wanda, my spicy little fantasy bunny. She was it! She was the one, my true love, that sexy little tail I dreamt of since I first saw her hop her hot little ass down the rabbit trail.

After our sweet morning mounting, I should have felt like a king. But I didn't. A few minutes after my dismount, something inside of me stirred, something foreign, something recently introduced. It felt like maggots squirming between my flesh and fur.

I staggered and steadied myself on a tree. My breathing was heavy. I tasted blood. And then I heard what sounded like a dead bird falling from the sky into a pile of leaves behind me. I searched the ground but saw no sparrow or bluebird or raven. I felt a cold breeze on my back as something wet ran down my shoulder blades.

Something's not right.

I remember thinking that.

Something is not fucking right.

I bent my arm around my back and ran my paw along my spine. It felt slick like the skin of Farmer Owsley's hairless cat after a heavy rain. I pulled my arm back and looked at my paw. It was drenched in blood.

You'd think at this point I would have panicked but I didn't. I was too young and dumb, too filled with a feeling of invulnerability to think anything bad could ever happen to me.

So I worked through all the many possibilities as to why my back was covered in blood. And why, underneath all that blood, I couldn't feel my fur, only exposed muscle.

Maybe I accidentally ate some of Farmer Owsley's magical lettuce. The last time that happened I got my penis stuck in one of Poppa's brown bottles. I thought it was a dolphin.

But that wasn't it.

I told myself that maybe some wicked little otter tossed a fat tomato at me. But that didn't make sense either.

None of it did.

I worked through a dozen demented and desperate explanations but none of them solved the puzzle.

So then I settled on the obvious, that I had imagined it all. Momentary psychosis.

Poppa always said that crazy ran in the family. Ignore the blood on your paw. Ignore what you thought you felt on your back.

Go ahead. Reach around. Feel it again. There ain't nothin' there but luxuriously soft white fur.

I often think of this moment, the moment just before I once again bent my arm behind my back and came face to face with reality, the last moment I was able to fool myself into believing nothing awful could ever happen to a young rabbit such as myself so long as I was safely ensconced in the Briar. That was the last moment I felt truly sane.

Anyway, to make a long, wretched story short, I once again reached my paw around my back. And once again I couldn't feel my fur. There was nothing but blood and sinewy exposed muscle.

"Oh momma. What's happening?"

And then I heard another bird fall from the sky and hit the ground. Only this time I not only heard it, I saw it. And it wasn't a bird. It was a patch of fur once wrapped around my shoulder. It slid off my body like a chunk of greasy burger meat off glass and plopped into the pile of leaves next to the first swath of fur.

It's hard to describe how I felt staring down at that bloody white mass of fuzz at my feet. It's seems like a goddamn lifetime ago. And since then I've done my best to come to terms with whatever it is I am now. But near as I can remember, the only thing I felt was anger. Rage.

I screamed and covered my eyes with my paws.

This isn't happening.

This isn't happening.

But when I pulled my paws away from my face, the skin on my skull stuck to them and peeled off with a squishy-squish sound.

I don't remember much after that. I ran home as fast as I could, shedding my fur with each frantic hop and bound.

The weird thing is that I never felt any physical pain. It was as if whatever connective tissue that held my fur to my flesh just up and evaporated.

A clean break.

When I finally crashed into my burrow, there was nothing left of my plush white coat. I looked like something that should be hanging in a butcher shop.

Poppa was sitting in his chair drinking the brown stuff when I blasted through the door and collapsed on the floor.

"Poppa! Poppa!" I screamed. "Help me Poppa!"

That's what I shouted, over and over again. "Help me Poppa!"

Only he didn't rush to my aid. I remember that. While I was writhing on the floor, completely skinless, not a patch of fur left on my body, Poppa kept his distance. Maybe he was afraid to catch whatever it was I had. Maybe he was in shock. Maybe he was too drunk to get a grip on the situation. Maybe he was trying to convince himself that what he was experiencing wasn't real, like I tried to do. Maybe he was trying to work through all of the possibilities that could explain away the cruel fucking reality before him.

Maybe, maybe, maybe.

I reached out to him with my Hellraiser hands.

"Help me Poppa."

I'd like to tell you that after discounting all of those made-up explanations, Poppa cradled me in his arms and told me it would all be ok, that he would fix whatever was happening.

But that's not what happened.

What happened is, I lost consciousness on the floor of our burrow, staring at Poppa as he stared back at me, draining another bottle. Calm as a fucking cucumber.

He didn't move an inch.

These are the crimson facts.

And I'm damaged.

And now I'm here, in this catastrophic city.

A true freak.

"Go south," the bum on the train told me.

After my excommunication from the Briar, after Poppa turned a cold shoulder, I didn't know where to go or what to do. So I hopped for miles until I ran into a big mechanical intestine charging down the gut of it all on rails of sorrow. And from out of the darkened bellies of one of the train cars I heard someone singing.

"Good morning America how are ya? Said don't you now me I'm your native son. I'm the train they call the city of New Orleans. I'll be gone 500 miles when the day is done."

I jumped into the open door as the metal thing slowed to a crawl and tumbled into a smelly bag of bones.

It's name, the bag of bones, was Bum Suk Lee. He was old like Farmer Owsley but the lines in his face were deeper, deep enough to plant crops in. And he was dirty. He was covered in a thick layer of dust and mud. And every now and then I spotted a worm poking its head from out of that layer of dirt that covered Bum Suk Lee.

"What's your name?"

"Rabbit."

"Well Rabbit, you look like shit. You look like a dog ate you and vomited you back up."

That hurt.

"But so do I," Bum Suk Lee said. "I weigh 110 pounds but got on 12 layers of sweaters and coats just to make me look like some kind of hulking buffalo of a beast. Out here on the rails, the only thing that matters is perception."

I shuffled away from him and settled against a far wall. I huddled in the darkness and wrapped my arms around the paper bag that held the remnants of my fur. Before I made my slow, sad trek out of the Briar, I spent hours retracing my steps, from Poppa's burrow to the redberry bush where I got it on with Honda Wanda, searching down all of the patches I shed, stuffing them in this paper bag of mine.

I didn't know what good they would do me. All I knew is that they were once part of me. They were mine. In this train, in the blackness, trapped with this strange human, a lumpy pile of foul clothing that stared at me as the thing in the night went bump, bump, bump, they were all I had left.

"Don't be scared Rabbit. I ain't gonna hurt you. Here, have some whiskey. You look thirsty."

He poured something in a tin cup and handed it to me. I took a sip. It tasted awful but warmed my insides and calmed my brain. He poured me another shot. I choked it down. And then another. And one for him. And one for me.

An hour later we were sprawled out on the floor staring at the passing blur of the world outside. I couldn't feel anything. And that was good enough for me. I figured I was good as dead—no family, no friends, no home. So I just sat there as the train rumbled over the countryside listening to Bum Suk Lee talk and talk and talk.....

"I tell you Rabbit, I done met a lot of weird motherfuckers on this here wagon but I ain't never met a skinned rabbit such as yourself. Now, you may worry about my reaction. I can see it in your eyes. Even with all that whiskey coursing through your blood, I can see the fear in you.

"It's good to be afraid. To you I must look like one scary motherfucker. Am I right? Don't imagine you've met too many people like me. Hell, have you ever even talked to a human before? Don't matter. What I want to tell you is that I don't mind that you look like a giant intestine. And I really don't care how you got that way. I hope you don't give a shit how I got the way that I got or why I'm sitting here on this train all by myself. Truth is, I haven't always been alone.

"Like I said, I done met a lot of different people on this wagon. I even seen me a girl who had a tail like an alligator. One day she hopped into the car I was sitting in, just like you done. Only she talked a whole lot. You don't talk much do you Rabbit? No worries. I suppose if I was in your shoes I wouldn't talk either. Don't feel bad. I don't mind doin' all the talkin'.

"So anyways, this girl had a tail like a gator. And we got on to talkin' and she told me her story. She said she was a backwoods girl from a poor family dominated by an abusive father and a momma so waxed on booze and pills it barely even registered that she had a daughter. But she did have a daughter. And her daughter was gorgeous, a real beauty queen, except for that hideous appendage growing out of the base of her spine.

"The boys didn't mind. They all had their way with her. Please don't judge. It's how she sought out comfort. But it always ended the same. The day after they bedded her down, they threw vicious insults at her. Called her every rotten name in the book. I suppose it made them feel better for what they done. But she was strong and she threw it right back at them. 'I may have a tail like an alligator but you fucked a girl with a tail like an alligator. I never had a choice. This is who I am. Can you say the same?'

"That shut them up and they always came back for more. But she wasn't into seconds. She was always after firsts. And when that tired little town of hers no longer provided any more firsts, she got the fuck out of Dodge. And that's when we met. She saw my train and jumped on in.

"At the time I was young, not like you see me now Rabbit. I wasn't so good looking. Don't think I've ever been good looking. Even as a baby. But I was young and that was good enough. I was also crazy. For such a young guy, I had done a lot of bad shit. Evil shit. Shit that will surely doom me to hell whenever the demons choose to take me. I've changed since then. I don't want you to worry. But back then, if someone like yourself rolled into my train car, a skinless rabbit, I would have chopped your head off and fried your innards over an open fire.

"But like I said. I'm a changed man. You're not scared are you? Naw, don't look like you are. Looks like your mind is a million miles away. Anyway, that gorgeous girl with the alligator tail rolled into my train car and she looked at me with those heart-stopping eyes of hers, those goddamn eyes, and she said to me, 'I'm Clara. Why don't you show me something new.'

"And that's what I did. I showed her things she ain't never imagined. I made sure every day we spent together was nothing but firsts. And she soaked it all in. I won't damage you with the details, but sure enough we broke just about every law, both man-made and heavenly-made. And she was into it all, body and soul.

"We jumped off the train at every stop and hit whatever town we landed in with everything we had. It was all blood and drugs and booze and money and sin. And then we jumped back on the train and moved on. We stripped down and she wrapped that tail of hers all around me as I sunk mine deep inside of her. She was always so sure of herself. That's what struck me. And what pulled me in and made me love her so. There was never a trace of doubt in her eyes. Something like that, it's intoxicating. So fucking rare. Don't know what she saw in me. Maybe I was just another first. And if I was, it was something to be proud of. My Alligator Angel.

"We rode these rails for two years together. And then she said something to me, something that made my heart stop. And when those words poured out of her mouth, upon hearing them, I don't think I've ever been happier. She said, 'Hey baby, you know how we talked about jumping off this train for good, finding a nice little house, killing its occupants and making a life for ourselves. I think I'm ready.' She didn't have to say another word.

"I kissed her and began to sharpen my knife. That night she fell asleep in my arms and I dreamt of all the possibilities, of hope and happiness and love, all those worldly gifts so foreign to my cruel heart. It seemed as if God busted a mind-gasket and accidentally blessed me. Even the ones on high make a mistake every now and then. But those mistakes are soon corrected.

"The next morning I woke up and found my angel in the corner of the car, her body rigid with death. Sometime in the middle of the night, she took my knife, chopped of her tail and stuck it straight down her throat. I was heartbroken. I wailed and wept for hours. I made love to her corpse for a week. And then I tossed her off into the brush somewhere in Alabama.

"I don't know why she did it. I've pondered over it for many a year and never came upon a satisfying answer. At first I thought maybe it was my ugliness that drove her to suicide. I thought that for a good long time. And that thought ruined me and left me thinking about the big death escape. But some time ago, after much pondering, I decided to believe in her love. I decided that to doubt her love was a great betrayal. I don't know why she did it. I suppose even love can't save us from our demons, whatever they may be. So I allowed her to go on her own terms without anger or self-loathing.

"After she died, my taste for riding the rails died as well. Fuck the goddamn train. Too many memories. So I jumped off at a stop in Mississippi and wandered into a dirt poor, slum-dumb town. I wanted to disappear. I wanted to die. I sat in a bar in that no-name town for a month trying to get my head around death and identity and love and loss. But there weren't any answers at the end of the bottle, just more fucking questions. Sure, on some nights, when I was deep into the drunk, I had a few moments of clarity, when I thought I had it all figured out. But they don't last too long, those moments of clarity. They scatter like cockroaches come the morning sun.

"On my last day in that piece of shit town, I found myself sitting on a street corner with my trembling fingers wrapped around a fifth of gin. I was in so much pain. I was delirious. I hadn't slept or eaten in weeks. I wanted to hurt myself. So I tightened my grip on the bottle and squeezed. Tighter and tighter. I wanted to break the neck and feel the shards of glass dig deep into my flesh and fracture my bones. And then I heard the scream of a child.

"To this day I can't really explain what happened, how I could have mistaken the neck of a child for the neck of a gin bottle. But there it is. I strangled a little girl in that godforsaken Mississippi town. I don't know how it happened, how it came to pass that the little girl came into my possession, into my murderous arms. But there it is. And there I was, staring down at the limp form of that beautiful auburn-haired angel. There was no one around us, no one to stop me. No answers, only a lifeless little body. I laid her on the street, gently, kissed her cheek and then I took off. I headed to the nearest tracks and jumped the first train that rolled by. That was 40 years ago. And I ain't never been off the rails since.

"I figured this here train was the safest place for me and my torment. I wanted to avoid all human contact. I was trying to protect myself from the world and the world from myself. I thought I was a monster. And maybe I am. I haven't figured it out yet. My God, that little girl.....

"I've come to terms with the fact that even upon my death I won't know what I am. But so it goes. You're probably wondering if I think about her, my Alligator Angel. Yeah Rabbit, I think about her every day, what could have been. It tortures me. But I find myself thinking just as much about that auburn-haired baby. I haven't figured out a whole lot in life. But what I do know is that being here on this train, everything moves. And when the world outside flies by at 150 miles per hour, it's damn near impossible to hurt the people who live in it. And they can't touch you either. So long as I make my home on this train, to the people out there in that stationary world, I may as well be living on Mars.

"And so my advice to you Rabbit, seeing how badly you've been scarred, is that you stay here with me on this train. You and me, we're the same. Our souls are damaged. Let's make our last stand here on these rails. There's nothing out there but hatred and ugliness."

Bum Suk Lee stopped talking. He looked at the brown paper bag clenched tight between my arms.

"What you got there?"

"It's my skin. It's all I got left of home."

And on came the tears.

Bum Suk Lee stared at me as I sobbed.

He knew.

The pain.

"You know what?" he whispered. "Forget about what I said. I don't know shit."

He walked to the edge of the open car door. He didn't say anything for several miles. When the train came to a stop in St. Louis, he breathed in deeply. The air was cool and clean. He took a swig off his whiskey bottle then turned to face me.

"There's still hope for you Rabbit. My story isn't yours. And I don't think the train life's for you. I've ruined enough innocence in my day. You want some advice, some real advice? You need to find somewhere you can settle down and figure shit out. That's what you need. And I think, after some time, once you've found some inner peace, that's when you'll be able to go home."

"But they kicked me out. They told me to never come back."

"Well Rabbit, fuck them. You get yourself well. You heal up. Get sane. And then you hop back on this train and I'll take you home myself. And once they see that you can't be broken, how strong and brave you are, they'll beg you to stay. It's all just one big test I bet. Maybe you're from some Amish rabbit tribe and this is your version of Rumspringa."

"Do you really think they'll take me back? I want to go home."

"Sure you do Rabbit. We all do. But you gotta get your feet wet first. Now listen, I like you. It don't faze me none that you look the way you do, all diseased like a leper. But most folk ain't as accepting as me. But there is one place that will accept a weird-looking cuss like yourself."

"Where's that?"

"New Orleans. Go to New Orleans. They'll look the other way. The plague is rampant there. You'll be just another monster in a monstrous city. That's how they'll see you. You'll be as good as invisible. Me and my Alligator Angel spent a lot of time there. We held a priest for ransom and no one even noticed. No one cared. We let him go after a week. No hard feelings. He invited us back to his rectory where we all got fucked up on wine and Valium. And he never once inquired about my girl's reptile tail. You're going through some hard times Rabbit. Any asshole can see that. But you need to embrace this moment and kick ass. And when you think you're ready to head on back home, you'll know where to find me. So how about it Rabbit?"

I wanted to go home. But I also wanted to prove to Poppa that I was strong. Maybe that's why he kicked me out. Maybe that's why he was so awful and mean. He thought I was weak. And maybe I am weak. Maybe that's why my fur fell off. I always thought I was strong, the strongest of all the young rabbits, invulnerable, impenetrable, invincible. But I was wrong. Look at me. What more proof do I need?

"So what's the story morning glory?" Bum Suk Lee asked. "What's it gonna be?"

I wiped my tears with one of my raw, exposed forearms. I stared outside as the world passed me by.

"I'm going to New Orleans."

GEMS SCRAPING THE EDGE

by X. C. Atkins

The curtain came apart and the chef came out and pointed at him.

"Service," he said.

Fenton stepped into the kitchen and the sound and heat and smell of the place hit him all at once. A goblin woman looked up at him as she scrubbed a mountain of plates, her eyes insane and frantic. The chef's back was to him and when he turned to face Fenton his forehead was beaded with sweat and he had a plate in each hand. He thrust them forth and licked his lips and said, "Table 26."

"Table 26," Fenton repeated robotically, and left that hellish world behind the curtain.

Fenton arrived at the aforementioned table and laid down one dish before a woman and the other in front of a man and said, "Shrimp and grits."

The man looked down at the dish and then his head jerked up at Fenton as if he'd laid before him the not-so-distant date of his death and simply said, "No."

"No? You didn't order the shrimp and grits?"

"Yes," he said then.

Fenton stared at him a moment longer and turned away before all kindness and courtesy left him, vanishing amongst the chaos of the swarming restaurant to leave the man with whatever he wanted to believe was true.

Across the dining room, the crash of wine glasses and champagne flutes, shattering everywhere, and a girl stood there, giggling stupidly, red faced, unable to draw any other expression but the acceptance of her own ineptitude.

An older gentleman smiled and shrugged. He must have thought she was cute.

It was over. The staff, mostly made of the kitchen, stood in the back around a table and in the center of a table was a bottle of Jameson and a stack of plastic cups and the chef poured the Irish whiskey into each cup and they held them up and took them down and some of them coughed and others closed their eyes. Fenton threw his cup away and said goodnight and left.

He rode his bike home the same way every night. The trees hung low and cast shadows. Streetlights seemed menacing. But there was an old cop with a thick mustache in front of a building Fenton passed, every night. And every night as Fenton passed him, the old cop nodded his head and waved. And Fenton would wave back. He liked that old cop.

He rode his bike up to an intersection. He heard something and braked. Out of the darkness, a black horse came plodding down the street. Even at night, its black mane seemed to shimmer with a type of terrible majesty. Atop the horse, rode a man, or else Fenton assumed so. The rider wore a helmet with a visor down, masking his face. He stared at Fenton a moment and a moment only and then they passed, as if the two had simply been some dreadful hallucination come in and out of his unacknowledged delirium.

Real or not, he rode his bike the rest of the way home bent forward like a gargoyle, pedaling like a mother.

Fenton unlocked both sets on the door and stepped inside and locked the door behind him. He turned on the light and took off his shirt and jeans and shoes and socks and sat down. He turned on some music from his laptop and closed his eyes. He let the relief seep into his bones. He wished he could fall asleep, just like that. But that was impossible. The adrenaline never leaves your body that quickly, no matter the hours you've invested. Not even when you believe with all your heart you have absolutely nothing else to give. There's always more to scrape from inside the barrel.

So he took out his phone and texted her.

He stared at the phone a moment after, foolishly expecting it to light up instantly with her response. He put the phone down and peeled himself out of the chair and went to the refrigerator. Nothing but a six pack of PBR, some tortillas, and spicy mustard. Fenton took one of the PBR's.

He drank beer and listened to music for a couple hours. He wondered where she was. What she could be doing. He wondered what movie his neighbor was watching. He went through all six beers. When he was done, he took a piss and brushed his teeth and looked in the mirror for a long time. Then he turned off the lights and got into bed as if it were a coffin.

Fenton closed his eyes and at that very moment his phone began to vibrate. He reached in the dark for it and looked at the screen.

It was her. The text stated nothing other than an address. He laid back in bed and closed his eyes.

Then he got out of bed and turned on the lights.

He was riding his bike in the dark again and the fear from before had been substituted with something else. A kind of wonder. A kind of excitement.

He rode fast and his headphones blared. Beads of every color hung from telephone wires and the gates of people's houses. He rode fast but always kept his eyes on the road. The city was old. The streets were treacherous and broke perpetually, giant potholes like gaping maws, sudden trolley tracks only half buried, street beneath street, gravel like quicksand. This was exciting too. This was the arduous path. And she would be there, standing at the end.

But when he rode over the train tracks, some measure of reality settled back into his secret thoughts. This effect always occurred, whenever Fenton rode over train tracks, anywhere. He didn't know at what age it had started happening, if it was because of watching too many movies or reading too many books. Whatever fantasy he'd grafted into the current affair, train tracks always, always stood for caution. A border was being crossed here and comforts from one place did not necessarily reside in another.

And then there was the address, hovering right above the red door.

Fenton nodded at a man with a green mohawk, sitting on the porch, legs dangling, and went inside the building.

Light wasn't for this place. Walls had been knocked out and ascents had been crudely constructed to take one to a second floor where people peered down like spying children from where platforms were absent. A built in cave with slumming bohemians fooling with gadgetry and wires, rasps of guitars and sound checks, a sparse crowd already beginning to form, hungry for any distraction, any hope. A couch made out of tires already occupied by lounging sirens with bored expressions, so old already in the blossom of their youth but for their glowing skin, abundant, as if summer were here. Fenton was wearing a jean jacket.

He turned to a black woman with milk cloud eyes who smiled when his gaze came upon her and she asked with soothing voice, "Drink?"

He asked for a beer and whiskey and saw the price from script off a piece of cardboard. Fenton gave her the money and she felt it and smiled and handed him the drinks. He said thank you and sincerely meant it.

Fenton passed all the people inside and went into the back of the building. Water streamed into a pool dug into the floor, full of lily pads and tiny darting fish, orange, black, and white. He sat down next to it and drank his beer. He listened to the water whisper.

This little sanctuary. He could have biked back home after a handful of minutes sitting there like that, floating in nostalgia and serenity, and been satisfied. Gone to sleep. Work the next inevitable and brutal double. And then she appeared, conjured in spite of any peaceful resolution.

"How we doing, Buddha?"

He turned around and there she was. She already had a beer in her hand. She was really a sight.

It was a shimmering green dress with feathers of every color everywhere. Crazy makeup and gold glitter. Her blond hair seemed to meld seamlessly with the crown she'd made for herself, this self-styled queen of pigeons. She held up her arms and the feathers hung as if they really were wings and she turned her head, closing her eyes and smiling. Fenton clapped.

"Amazing. Amazing," he said.

She helped him up. He stared at her, speechless.

"It was a big party and everyone was dressed up but then it just got stale and, well, it was time to leave. I like your jean jacket," she said.

"Thanks."

"I'm glad you came," she said.

"Well," he said, looking down, "I'm glad too."

They stood there, smiling, silent, the universe on the verge of imploding.

"Have you been out back yet?"

Fenton shook his head.

"Come on."

He followed her outside and up spiral stairs of metal that went up into a night become cool, a bonfire licking upwards in the expanse of the yard where someone played a ghostly banjo and girls hoola-hooped. He stepped over some sleeping body and walked across a net of rope suspended in the air, looking down, already too late to second guess, the way she pressed on so resolutely canceled the existence of concepts like alarm and doubt.

A group of vagrants sat on a platform there in the sky passing around a doobie. They joined them as if they were old friends. The stars looked wonderful.

The doobie came to him and he didn't ask. It hit powerfully.

"Take your time," someone said.

An older man next to him was looking into the sky. There a plane blinked down at them but they could not hear it.

"Cadillacs swimming in a dead static tv sky," he said. "And us. Gems scraping the edge. All of us."

Fenton looked at him and didn't stop until he caught himself drooling. Embarrassed, he wiped his mouth. He hadn't realized the whole of him was being sucked into that old man's soul. As if he was just breathing Fenton in. He moved away from the man but he looked back at Fenton with no malice and Fenton knew he had only to be more careful with his love. He remembered the rail road tracks. He was out of the man's spell then, but when he looked around the party, she was no longer among them.

There was nowhere to go but onward. But he was alone.

He thought about leaving right then. Something told him tonight was not yet over.

He stepped past the group, apologizing, holding onto the netting, for the first time realizing how high up in the air they were, the over-flowing confidence cut in half with her disappeared somewhere. Could he even find her? Fenton had no idea where the fuck he was himself. I'm going to fall and splatter my brains, he thought. Fenton pushed that out of his head. No rearview mirrors, is what he made his new mantra. No rearview mirrors.

He climbed a ladder into some bunker. The place was candle lit. She sat on the ground Indian-style with some other guy. She looked at him and smiled.

"Hey," Fenton said.

She stood up and took his hand. They went back down, but down a different ladder, or it seemed like it. But he'd found her. He wasn't alone.

They were walking through some other spider web tunnel and Fenton stopped and said, "What are we doing here?"

"Let's go swimming."

"What just happened up there?" he asked her.

"I'm a bumblebee," she told him.

"What?"

"He told me. My spirit animal is a bumblebee. Do you know what yours is?"

Fenton looked up into the sky. There was the moon, big as hell. He resisted the urge.

"Where are we going?"

"We're going swimming."

"Now?"

"Now."

They returned to the earth from the maze in the sky and ran through the cracked-open house, past blaring sound and bouncing bodies and guilty light. The green mohawk still out there, smoking a cigarette, nodding, ever watchful, days and storms passing by, nails turning yellow, and there would always be others.

She jumped into a four door wagon type car.

"My bike," he said.

"Put it in the back," someone yelled.

He got his bike and lifted the backdoor and angled it inside. Then he got in the backseat with her. The car started but Fenton felt off suddenly, like he could feel the illusion beginning to dissipate. Something inside him was beginning to feel abrasive and raw. Then he saw a bear was driving.

Or it was someone in a bear costume.

"You ever seen that movie Finding Nemo?"

The bear looked at Fenton when he said this.

"Yeah."

"This is the part where Nemo rides with the turtles. Except I'm a bear. Well, actually my name's Todd."

Someone handed something back to her and she handed one to Fenton.

"I have to work a double tomorrow," he said.

"Then you probably shouldn't," she said.

He looked up and the bear was looking at him. The bear had a smile on his face. His eyes were so huge.

Fenton took the pill.

She laughed, holding her hand in front of her mouth. Her head went all the way back when she laughed. It was a good thing to watch. He wanted to strangle her neck. Out of a type of love. Ha ha.

They crossed more train tracks.

They played the music so loud. Fenton could feel the bear looking at him from the rearview. He didn't know whether it was out of judgment or that he may have been happy for them. Fenton didn't care. He couldn't keep his hands off of her. Her breath was some intoxicating mix of cigarettes and huckleberry. Her neck was a pillow that turned into a bed that turned into a dream.

Air rushing by, bass pulsing from every side, each crack and crater in the road like a space ship kissing an asteroid. Everything inside of him seemed to be feeling the world for the first time. And it was nowhere near the first time, but what no one told you was there many, many worlds, and you have the chance to live in several, maybe not always or all the time, but in nights like this, days or mornings like this, fleeting, a song you never hear again but forever recall the melody. He put his arm out the window and watched it turn into a snake slithering up into the black universe. Like he had a place to go. Like home was out there somewhere.

No. Then he knew for sure, none of it was true. There wasn't a way he or anybody could know that was true.

They got out of the car like zombies and followed the bear and Fenton realized there were more than the two of them and that bear. They went through a gate and he could hear it. Lights came on. A pool. Someone ran straight for it. Even just the sound of a splash time-gated every single one of them to childhood.

Fenton was doing a Spider-Man crawl on the walls of the pool because he hadn't yet learned how to swim. It was his aunt's pool and he was in love with her.

She was so beautiful. Except she wasn't his aunt. She just liked him to call her that. She had big fluffy hair like a cloud had attached itself to her head, but her hair was black. And big dark sunglasses. He wanted to believe the eyes behind those sunglasses held nothing but love for him.

When she smiled, with those red lips, Fenton wished he could grow years in seconds so in hours she'd let him kiss her.

He remembered as they'd had arrived, the man Fenton's mother said was his aunt's boyfriend was leaving. He left on a motorcycle. He was wearing a black helmet. Fenton never saw his face. The visor was down. Fenton hated him. He knew the man couldn't be good for her. But there's no way to articulate those types of feelings when you are a child. Not without bursting.

Everyone left the pool to go inside to eat. Fenton stayed out there, holding onto the wall and letting his legs float in the water. He was flying somewhere. Earliest memories of solitary wanderlust. These things stay with you for the rest of your life.

He let loose the wall and then he drifted too far. He was adrift. But he hadn't yet learned how to swim.

He started to drown. It was the most desperate, loneliest feeling. He submerged. Light twinkled from above. He could hear people yelling. Someone splashed into the water. His brother saved his life that day. Fenton cried so hard into his arms. They all held him.

Fenton was being pulled back up and was lifted out of the water and laid down. When he opened his eyes, dazed, just above him was the bear. Todd. Those big eyes and indestructible smile. I will trust you forever.

The sun was coming up.

"I have to go to work," Fenton told the bear, still looking up at him.

"Let me take you home," Todd said.

And he did. The bear dropped him off. Awkwardly, Fenton hugged him. His wet, bear arms wrapped around him.

"Thank you," Fenton told him.

"Have a good day at work," Todd the bear said. He lingered a moment as Fenton removed his bike from the back, and then rode off.

Fenton went inside his apartment and brushed his teeth. He had ten minutes to get to work.

He was ten minutes late.

He locked up his bike and as he did he felt his phone vibrate in his pocket. He took it out and read the message.

Good luck today, she'd sent.

He smiled, even though it hurt to.

He came in through the back gate. His manager sat there, smoking a cigarette. He looked up at Fenton from his glasses.

"You're late," he said. "Did you go for it last night?"

"I did."

"Did you get it?" he asked.

"I don't know."

He stood up and came up very close to Fenton. His manager had always seemed a diminutive character since his employment at the restaurant but at that moment he seemed to loom over him.

"Nothing you do is new," he said.

Those words seemed to pound on top of Fenton like a Super Mario mallet.

"Go inside and get dressed and get ready for work. Get your shit together. Because we're gonna get fucked today."

And they did. Get fucked. But they made it through. As you always do, one way or the other. Whether it end in victory, inconsequence, or misery. You always make it through. Until, finally, you find a way out. And then your days will never be like these. And that's another thing you have to prepare for, or settle for, or be grateful for. More train tracks. More swimming pools. If you're really lucky, kisses in the sky.

SOLSTICE

by Amy Conner

There's no such thing as last call, not at The Tombs.

After Traci spends all night pouring drinks for losers, freaks and hopelessly lost tourists in the French Quarter dive, it's good to go have a few drinks somewhere else before going home to sleep the rest of the day away. As her shift is ending this June morning, a few sounds like not enough.

"Lookin good, sugar lips." It's Dwight, one of The Tomb's resident drunks, one of the ones who never seem to go away. He never leaves a tip either, although he always seems to have plenty of crumpled dollar bills for the video poker machine. "Hey honey, where y'going?"

"Home." It's a lie. Traci is over every man walking the planet, not just creeps like Dwight.

"Want shome comp'ny?" Dwight's bloodshot eye winks in a puffy leer—his sexy look, one that might have worked in another life, the one he had a thousand bottles of cheap rum ago. But Traci hasn't brought a man home to her apartment in two years, not since Morgan, and that's the way she wants it. Besides, it's *Dwight*.

"No." Traci cashes out fast. "Bye, Rae-Lynn." She stuffs her tips in her purse, lights up the last Camel in her pack and slams through the pass-through. She's free, out from behind the plywood bar.

Traci's worked the late shift at The Tombs since she came to New Orleans. It had been six months on the road with her then-boyfriend Morgan and she was dead broke and hungry, so hungry she couldn't be picky about things like hours, shifts or health insurance. She'd been following his dream of cashing in big time at the Black Jack tables, driving cross-country from one Harrah's casino to the next in Morgan's Camry.

"You're gonna love New Orleans." Morgan, sure that he was going to stage a come-back in the Big Easy. "Whole fucking city's like living in a fairy tale."

The fairy tale ended in New Orleans with a hiss of dissipated hope like a collapsed balloon. "It's not working out, babe." Three days after their arrival, Morgan moved in with the stripper he'd met in a tittie bar on Bourbon Street. No money, no Morgan, no life, and so Traci fell back on bartending, but what she hadn't realized was how the job would screw up her plans for getting a real job, a straight day job, so she could finally go to night school to become a paramedic. She hadn't realized how she'd lose her days to the lingering shadows of the shift, to the screwed-up circadian rhythms of her thirty year-old body. Working from midnight until eleven in the morning when perennially late Rae-Lynn comes in to take over, Traci leaves to face a sharp-edged and tiresome reality outside The Tomb's doorway of fluttering Visqueen strips.

And always, always she needs a drink.

Standing on Decatur Street this morning with her half-smoked cigarette, Traci knows she ought to go home, but home is almost never where she goes. Wired from the combination of boredom and vigilance necessary to survive the graveyard shift, all she wants to do is hide from the daylight's glassy glare. She knows she should go home to shave her long legs, dye her leaf-brown hair to cover the gray that's been creeping into her hair-line since her thirtieth birthday, give herself a facial to combat the toll cigarettes, booze and no sleep exacts. She could clean the bathroom, take a walk, buy groceries, do the normal.

But this morning, like always Traci is going to stop in at the Solstice, a nicer bar than the Tombs that's on the way back to her shitty apartment in Treme. At the Solstice, a morning's eye-opener or two turns into an afternoon's series of pick-me-ups. Around 3:00 the construction workers, off-shift waitresses and lawyers start to wander in, the bullshit back-and-forth begins, and so with only hours left until her shift at The Tombs commences, sometimes Traci doesn't go home at all but finds herself back behind the bar in an endless loop of alcohol, her and the regulars like Dwight somehow making it through till morning.

Even after she puts on her sunglasses, this morning's edges are sharper than ever. In addition to the litter of go-cups, tamale wrappers, torn lost-dog flyers and bus exhaust, to Traci's irritation there's a dense crowd of tourists blocking the sidewalk. Traci tries to elbow her way through the early Voodoo Tour, but the heat-stunned, sweating folks from Des Moines, or Memphis, or Las Cruces are crowding the pavement like a flock of obese hens carved from Crisco.

"Get a fucking permit, Wide Load," Traci mutters under her breath. She's learned what the locals know: tours trump her right to the pavement by virtue of their mass. A thankfully tourist-free block later, she turns left onto Governor Nicholls Street, barely avoiding a dog on a string, a pile of dog shit and an old lady who's likewise smoking a cigarette. She's wearing a faded housecoat falling open to reveal a nylon nightie, and her left arm is immobilized in a dirty cast.

"'Scuse me," Traci says, but the old lady doesn't answer, nor does she move out of the way. In a cracked falsetto, she's singing with the calliope music skirling down the street from the steamboat on the river, singing to the dog, a squatting mess of matted fur. The only way Traci can tell which end is which is by the pink collar on one end and what's coming out the other.

"That happy tune in your step, lah-dah-ti-dah," the old lady shrills, her voice a ravage of nicotine. "Hmm, hmm dah-dah-*dah*, on the sunny side of the street."

Whoever wrote that song never lived in New Orleans, Traci thinks. The sunny side of the street feels like death by

Crock-Pot this steamy morning, but the bar is in sight at last. She ducks into the shade of the crape myrtle trees lining the sidewalk in front of the Solstice. Traci's learned to loathe the smell of crepe myrtle blossom, the harbinger of summer. She figures that the drifts of white, lavender and watermelon-colored flowers on the sidewalk are like the first flurries of snow in Maine—a tangible reminder that good weather never lasts long enough.

Traci walks inside the Solstice where late morning's slanting light just penetrates the open doorway in an oil-spill of hot yellow, but the rest of the long bar is blessedly dark, cool with air-conditioning. Ancient ceiling fans the size of semi tires rotate overhead, stirring the air that smells of bleach above the just-mopped white marble floors.

Bobby O., her favorite bartender, should be coming on shift by now. Traci takes off her sunglasses and the bar's dark shadows turn to a grainy light, a badly focused photograph in a dusty frame. The tall barstool tips when she sits and for an instant the wall of softly gleaming bottles in front of her seems to slide sideways like the deck of a ship in a swelling sea. Traci blinks.

"Bobby O.?" Nobody answers in the empty bar. Traci raises her voice, since maybe he's back in the kitchen. "Hey, gimme a..."

For a moment, all the possibilities present themselves: a Tequila Sunrise, a Screwdriver, a Greyhound, a Bloody Mary—something with a little nutritional content—but then Traci remembers the depressingly flat fold of bills in her purse. This time of year it's losers like Dwight all night long, the tourists rarely making it to the lower Quarter in June because it's too damned hot even to get lost.

Looks like a PBR, then. That's Pabst Blue Ribbon, the cheapest beer the Solstice has to offer. Hey, at least it's cold; no small thing when the morning's mercury has already reached ninety-two and is still climbing like a snake in a rubber tree.

"Bobby?" The bar is silent. "Where the fuck are you, dude?"

There's no answer. It seems Bobby O.'s professionally half-shaven, handsome self is MIA. He must be upstairs above the bar checking the inventory, since the garnishes—lemons, limes and orange slices—are prepped, the olives and cherries still glistening from their bath in the gallon jars under the bar. This is a hell of a thing. All Traci wants is a damned beer. With a yawn, she gets up and buys another pack of Camels from the cigarette machine. Returning to the barstool, she resigns herself to wait.

Having time on her hands sucks. Traci doesn't want to think this morning. She doesn't want to find herself wondering what Morgan's up to now, she doesn't want to think of her parents on the phone last week, asking her when she's going to come to her senses and move back to Kentucky. She especially doesn't want to think about how, at thirty years old, she feels like she's fifty—tired, dry and used up. No, when she's got a drink in front of her she doesn't have to think about any of that, so where the hell is Bobby O.? Her watch says it's 11:35. That can't be right. She left work at 11:30 because Rae-Lynn had been late again. It's a solid ten-minute walk from the Tombs to the Solstice, even keeping to the shady side of the street and fighting her way through the tourists, and since she sat down she's smoked two cigarettes already. Her watch must be broken. Traci gives her wrist a shake but the watch continues to tick off the seconds as it always does.

"Cheap piece of shit." It's been a long damned time to wait for a drink by any measure. Traci should leave and buy a six-pack at Habeeb's Quick-Stop on the corner, head on home and do something on her list for a change.

And then, just before she picks up her cigarettes and sunglasses to go, down in the dark at the end of the bar she glimpses a half-seen figure. Traci swivels on the rickety stool to give Bobby a piece of her mind, keeping a customer waiting so long, and the room tilts again on the barstool's uneven feet. The figure pauses.

"Crap," Traci mutters under her breath. It's not Bobby O. It's The Ghost.

The Ghost's hat, a sweat-stained leather job with a high peak and low, wide brim, almost conceals a rodent face, only the receding chin with its meager crop of long whiskers visible underneath it. His bony shoulders in a ripped Mega Death t-shirt shrug at Traci's glance, as though her eyes on him are like a swarm of mosquitoes. The Ghost's lower half is hidden behind the bar so she can't see what else he's wearing, but she can guess. He's got on the same dirty pair of sneakers bursting along their seams, held together with raveling duct-tape. Worn jeans will be hanging off his prominent hipbones, held up with what has to be a knotted dog-leash. Even though he's been working here for a while, the Solstice regulars call him The Ghost because nobody can be bothered to learn his name.

Because they're all ghosts, the anonymous guys hired to do the heavy lifting for the bar's Mexican kitchen, El Puerco Negro—which is a joke because nobody's Mexican back there. The Ghosts lug buckets of ice to the bar from the ice-machine in the alley, hump cases of salsa from the Sysco delivery van and mop the floors. They also get stiffed on pay-day when the bar's owner, Norris, docks them for the crummy Mexican food they eat on their feet. Norris is from Istanbul and was formerly known as Al-Nouri. Every item on the abbreviated menu comes straight out of the Sysco vats and everything tastes the same: foreign and strange. All the regulars revile the Turkish Tacos. Nobody orders them unless they're so blitzed they can't even see the numbers on their cell phones to order out for anything else. This latest incarnation of The Ghost is more down-and-out than many of that lost tribe of delivery men and bar-backs. He must have taken the whole Ghost-thing to heart more than most because like a spook he flickers on the edges of your vision, sliding around corners, vanishing only to reappear in places you don't expect—like the ladies' bathroom.

Traci looks away, bored and a little repulsed. When she turns back again a half-beat later, The Ghost is still there.

"Where's Bobby?" she demands.

The Ghost shrugs again before he disappears around the stacked cases of beer, heading for the kitchen. Probably going into the alley for ice.

Ice sounds wonderful. Damn, she's thirsty. Traci doesn't really want to go home, but this waiting is getting ridiculous. The bottles behind the bar twinkle agreement with her that this is indeed ridiculous, that she deserves a drink if only for waiting for it so long. Why not? It's not like she's going to skip out on her bill, right? She knows where the beer lives.

So Traci gets off the stool and walks behind the bar, just like she works there. But without thought, it seems, instead of reaching into the cooler for a PBR her hand goes right to the square-shouldered bottle of Bushmills. Much, much later, Traci will wonder—why Bushmills? She never drinks it in the summer. Irish whiskey is for the long, dark afternoons of winter, when the north wind stalks across Lake Pontchartrain in bitter ill will, when the Mississippi is fogged with bad news from up-river and even as she pours herself a double shot into the bar-glass, she knows the Irish will taste like diesel because Irish always does.

Only it doesn't. The whiskey runs headlong down her throat in pure, amber valor, setting her up for the next double. Why not? Traci thinks again. She pours another quick glass. A bonfire ignites in her stomach, but the third shot bolts through her veins like a horse that's smelled the green hills of home. Traci's knees buckle, her hands grab the bar.

"Whoa," she breathes. She needs to get back to the other side of the bar if she doesn't want to get caught passed out back here. There's not enough tip-money to pay for three double shots of call-brand whiskey, either. Getting the Bushmills returned to its place on the top row is a wobbly, bottle-clanking ordeal but somehow she gets it done.

God, Traci wonders. What's got into her?

Whiskey! her impaired synapses scream. "Steady," she whispers, trying to feel where her feet have gone. It's a long, bar-hugging way to the other end, past the beer cooler, the wine rack and the ice-bin. Overhead, the ceiling fans seem to hum at a higher register, a counterpoint to the wailing thread of calliope music floating inside through the open door.

Traci has managed to round the end of the bar and is back in customer territory when her traitor knees turn to sand. She's falling halfway to the floor when a strong hand catches the waistband of her jeans, hauling her back upright onto her wobbly Sketchers.

The Ghost. He's the one holding her up. The reek of stale beer, sweat and clothes that haven't seen a washing machine in weeks surrounding her, Traci's face is buried now in a neck ringed with beads of dirt. She clings to The Ghost's bony shoulder anyway and gasps, one hand holding desperately to the dog-leash on his non-existent hips because he's frog-marching her like a twenty-gallon bucket of ice down the length of the bar. What? Has The Ghost turned into a bouncer now?

"Put me down," Traci mumbles into the grimy hollow of his neck. "I can walk." Her lips are numb, the whiskey a partisan Irish riot in her brain. But instead of getting dumped on her ass outside the Solstice's doors, though, she finds herself hoisted back onto her bar stool again, the world a-slant and precarious.

Without a word to her, the Ghost does that fade-thing and is gone.

Bleary Traci braces herself on her hands, looks down and, like a magic trick, there on the bar in front of her is a styrofoam to-go box full of Turkish Tacos. Food. The Ghost must have forgotten his delivery order there when he picked her up back there, keeping her off the floor. Oh man, food is what she needs right now, no matter that the taco shells are fast collapsing into soggy, corn-meal diapers stuffed with fried meat of steaming dubiousness, wilted lettuce and globs of cheese.

Overhead, the ceiling fan's whir has become a penny whistle, singing of county fairs and dancing under the stars as Traci throws her hair over her shoulder and digs in. Gorging herself with both hands, the grease running down her chin, strong-flavored chunks of mysterious vegetation pass almost unchewed between her back teeth. After the first two tacos, she's satiated, full of strange flavors, odd textures and Sysco salsa, but she can't stop until the to-go box is empty. Traci licks her greasy hands, sucking the last taste from her fingers.

Slowly, the world resolves its mad spin and comes to rest underneath her. Gradually, the ceiling fans' song returns to simple air-moving. Traci burps a long musical belch and she tastes Turkish Tacos all over again. She props her head in her hands. Her eye-lids droop. Outside the open doors, the calliope plays something familiar, something just out of reach.

Grab your coat and get your hat,
Leave your worries on the doorstep,
Life can be so sweet…

"On the sunny side of the street," someone sings in off-key good cheer. Traci raises her head with an effort, her hair in her face. It's Bobby O. at last, his white t-shirt an immaculate smudge coming towards her from the dark end of the bar.

"Hey, Trace," Bobby O. says, grabbing a couple of napkins on the way. "Here." He drops them in front of her. "What can I get you, babe?" Bobby's looking at the empty, grease-rimmed styrofoam box, his eyebrows raised, an amused grin not quite covering his disgust. "What y'doing, eating this shit? Come on—choose life, girl!"

"I, uh…gotta go." And Traci burps again, but this time the Irish has joined the Turkish Tacos in multi-cultural solidarity. She's got to get out of here.

"Later," Traci slurs. She holds on to the back of the bar stool for a beat, getting her sea-legs under her, then staggers across the marble floor. The open door is leagues away, but Traci gets outside to the sidewalk in a little under an hour, or so it seems. The calliope is playing "Camptown Races" now and the sunny side of the street has moved to the other side, not the Solstice side, the light slanting from the west above the roofs of the French Quarter. How did she lose what's left of the afternoon? A glance at her broken watch tells her it's an impossible 3:16, a full six hours until sunset on this longest day of the year.

Under the green-dappled shade of the crepe myrtle trees, Bobby O. unlocks the doors to the Solstice to start the morning shift. He whistles the tune the calliope is playing, the same tune the old lady down the block is singing to her dog. Life can be so sweet. She's wearing a cast on her right arm now, and a different house-coat. The nightie is the same.

"Hey Angie," Bobby O. calls. "How's the arm?"

"Mendin," she answers. "Hurry up, you damned dog." The mess of fur snuffles the base of the lamp post in damp, blind obsession.

"Gotta watch your step, old gal," Bobby says. He laughs. "Y'only got two arms, you know. Getting to be a yearly thing with you, huh? Left arm last summer, right one now?"

"Fuck off, sonny," Angie growls, snapping her cigarette butt into the gutter.

"Litter-bug." Bobby O. props the Solstice's glass-paned doors open and cool air washes out onto the sidewalk that's covered with crepe myrtle blossom. Back inside, he commences the prep work. Scents of oranges and lemons fill the air of the bar, redolent with pith and oil.

"The sunny side of the…." Bobby O. hums and then he puts down the knife, eyes narrowed. A woman's figure is backlit in the doorway, a young woman with a baby stroller. There's a baby, too—a fat, solemn-faced baby with a lot of brown hair.

"Trace?" Bobby O. says, mildly incredulous. "Zat you, babe?"

The young woman rolls the stroller across the cool marble floor. "Hey, Bobby O." Traci is wearing a paramedic's uniform, her long, leaf-brown hair pulled back into a shining horse-tail. She smiles, and somehow the bar seems brighter as she lifts the baby out of the stroller. "Meet Preston," she says, settling the baby on her hip.

"He yours?"

"All mine."

"So how you been, girl?" Bobby asks. "Nobody seen you for, what, a year now?"

"A year to the day. You believe that?" Traci answers. She strokes the baby's cheek with a finger-tip.

"You still working down to The Tombs?" Bobby O. picks up a bar napkin and places it in front of her on the bar. "PBR, right?"

"No, and…no," Tracy says. "I quit working at that shit hole about nine months ago. I'll have an O.J., okay? Preston's breast-feeding," she says unself-consciously. The baby gurgles, a sound almost swallowed by the shush-shush-shush of ceiling fans overhead.

"You up and quit, huh?" Bobby grabs the big jug of orange juice from under the bar.

"Yeah," Traci says, "Sort of. Once I figured out I was pregnant, I couldn't take the freaking Tombs another minute. Walked out of there, made a gyno appointment and registered for night school all in one day."

Bobby O. pours Traci a big plastic cup of juice. "On the house, babe. Welcome back to the Solstice. You looking good, by the way."

And she is: Traci's skin is creamy, lambent as though a candle glows just beneath the surface. Her brown eyes are clear, the whites almost blue with health. "Thanks," she says.

"You want to get together later, catch up?" Bobby eyes her with real appreciation.

"No, thanks." Tracy checks her watch, a small golden Rolex. "I'm meeting Travis in a few."

"Oh. He the..." Bobby jerks a thumb at the baby in her arms.

"No," Traci says. "Travis was my gynecologist. Now he's my boyfriend." The silence hangs. Traci sips her juice. "Thanks for the O.J., Bobby." She clears her throat. "Um. Hey, any chance The Ghost is still around?"

"Which Ghost we talking 'bout, hon?" Bobby is busy, back to slicing lemons. "There's always one somewhere."

Traci's eyes slide away. She sets the plastic cup on the bar and wipes her hand on her blue slacks. "You know, the guy working here last June? The really skinny Ghost with the hat?" Her voice is lowered now, maybe more than a little nervous. She looks over her shoulder, down into the dark end of the bar, towards the kitchen. The baby shifts in her arms, looking up at her with opaque blue eyes one shade darker than the color of Wedgewood china.

"*That* Ghost." Bobby O. laughs. "Babe, that one took off, oh, right after you dropped out of sight." He smiles at the baby. "Sometimes you lose a good ghost."

There's another silence after that. "Well, dude—it's been great." Traci reaches into the diaper bag hanging from the stroller, retrieves her wallet. "Here." She puts a couple of twenties on the bar. "I want to close out my tab."

Bobby O. looks at the twenties. He looks at Traci. "You don't have a tab here, darlin—you know we don't run 'em for anybody. Bad for business."

But Traci is tucking the baby back into the stroller, handling the straps and quick-release clamps and padded nylon harness like a pro. "Oh, it's an old one, been on my mind a lot lately. Take care, Bobby O."

The doorway is a lacework of sun, brilliant-streaming through the weft of trees. Traci pushes the stroller outside onto the sidewalk, shading her eyes.

Memory has faded. Traci almost doesn't remember wandering back to her apartment after leaving the Solstice last year, and for sure she doesn't remember passing out on her stained couch with the windows open to the pitiless heat in a desperate plea for a breeze. She doesn't remember anyone visiting her during the shortest night of the year. Nobody carried her to bed, nobody pushed her long, brown hair off her slack-mouthed face and kissed her tenderly. The taste of honey, whiskey and flowers, the delicious ache between her legs the next day—all of that forgotten as soon as day dawned again in New Orleans and the heat drove dreams away.

Traci picks up a handful of scattered white blossom from the sidewalk, crushing it to her nose. "Crepe myrtle, Preston," she says. She sprinkles a fragrant shower over the baby's dark crown of hair. "That means it's summer."

The stroller bumps down the curb, Traci pulls the canopy over her baby to shade him from the glare and steps out into the white-hot light of the sunny side.

RIVER FOG

by Dave Holt

It was 4 AM on a balmy January morning in New Orleans and I had just finished another unremarkable graveyard shift gig playing piano at the Apple Barrel on Frenchmen Street. I kept up my Friday night gigs at the Barrel, playing for the drunken tourists in their Hawaiian shirts, 5 pounds of beads and Nikon cameras hanging around their necks, while they sent texts on their cell phones and waited to eat at Adolfo's, a romantically corky Italian restaurant upstairs. It's one of the many hidden-away nooks in New Orleans that tourists will wait hours to get seated at. And, while they were waiting, they were mine. They would be waist deep into drunk, coming and going until about 2 AM when the last diners staggered down the stairs and out into the Frenchmen Street chaos. They were always an easy crowd, slobbering along with *When the Saints Go Marching In and I Wish I Was in New Orleans.* There were a lot worse gigs in this town, and I'm not a particularly flashy player. I'm more of a story teller sitting behind a piano. These people were so happy to be in New Orleans, I could easily have spent half the night just telling them stories like the one about the legendary Coco Robicheaux, who died just a year earlier at this very bar, ten feet from the piano.

An icon of New Orleans for years as both a blues musician and voodoo priest, he was a sight to behold with waist long hair falling over his shoulders, numerous tattoos, necklaces of bones and feathers and mystical amulets, his cowboy hat and snake skin boots. Most nights Coco could be found sitting on the bench out front dispensing advice, stories and swamp folklore to anyone who cared to listen. Supplying Coco with tequila would always result in his waxing prophetic. He never charged me for spiritual advice or the voodoo blessings he gave me with gris-gris bags and handmade bracelets and necklaces.

He had spent most of the day he died with his daughter and grandchildren before returning to New Orleans and his regular barstool at the right end of the bar at the "Barrel." He had been going on about what a great day he had spent with his family. Everyone was commenting on how well he looked. He had just ordered a round of tequila in plastic cups, his favorite drink, for everyone at the bar. His last words, spoken to the bartender's back were, "This round's on me." When the bartender turned back around with the drinks, Coco was face down on the bar, dead.

Word of his passing spread through New Orleans faster than a politicians promise on Election Day. Everyone was shocked that Coco was gone but no one was at all surprised by his last words. For the next week the Barrel was packed with mourners who had known Coco for years, along with the curious folks who had just learned of his legend. Frenchmen Street saw a second line parade every night that week. New Orleans sent Coco, one of its favorite sons, off in grand style as only New Orleanians can. It was never quite the same around the Barrel without Coco around. There's a hand lettered sign hanging behind the bar that says "Coco Robicheaux – you were always here, you're still here and you'll always be here." I'm sure I've heard that gravelly voice in the crowd many times since he passed.

I checked my cell phone and it was almost 3 AM. The professional drinkers started to slither in, one by one, to grab "their" stools at the bar. It's still a little strange to see someone else sitting at the end stool where Coco used to hold court. This crowd was easy too. They just wanted some music for distraction so they wouldn't picture themselves drinking to death in a silent blue haze of cigarette smoke, coughing up pieces of their lungs while they slugged down shots of cheap booze. Sometimes they even mumbled some unintelligible mumbo jumbo to me buried in stale whiskey and cigarette breath. All I had to do was pretend I was listening to them and say "Yeah, you right," a couple of times and I became their best friend and confidant, even if their eyes couldn't focus on my face. They were always good for buying me drinks and they were loose with the tip money; bless their clogged-artery hearts. That night was a little odd because I usually at least recognized most of the serious late-night drinkers if not knew them by name. The joint was half-filled with unfamiliar strangers that looked a little seedier than usual. Long greasy hair and beards with beads and stuff woven in. A lot of guys wore bandanas and raggedy pants with bare feet, mostly keeping to themselves. I noticed they had less than their share of teeth and more than their share of tattoos.

By 4 AM they had pretty much either staggered out or passed out or both and I was ready to go. I emptied the tip jar and cashed out with Jimmy the bartender. I stuffed ten bucks in my pocket and left the rest of the money in a zipped up bank bag with Jimmy. Carrying a wad of cash through the French Quarter in the middle of the night was not a good idea. I might have been born at night, but not last night. I'm not a three piece suit and necktie kind of guy who would have looked worth holding up but I'd come back in the daytime to pick up my money.

After bumping fists with Jimmy, I headed out on my usual route to Canal Street to catch the first streetcar of the morning heading Uptown to take me home. As I walked out the door of the Barrel I plunged into a lake of fog and a sea of empty space. The fog was as thick as grits and I couldn't make out the other side of Frenchmen Street. The air was saturated with prayers and dreams. The pavement and street were wet but it wasn't raining. There was a warm breeze blowing from the direction of the Mississippi, pushing the thickest river fog I had ever seen. Sounds were muffled as if I had cotton stuffed in my ears. I couldn't actually make out people, just groups of shadowy figures that moved about in twos and threes.

I turned right and headed up Frenchmen towards Royal Street and one of my favorite haunts, the Royal Street Inn and Bar, or, as it's called around here, the R Bar. One of the better B and B's in the Marigny, although here it's not a bed and breakfast but rather a bed and beverage place. Nice rooms upstairs at the inn, and a bad-ass bar downstairs. They don't serve breakfast at the R Bar, but, on Monday nights for ten bucks you can get a haircut and a shot. They do have a decent pool table and an infamous juke box. I usually stopped by to play a couple racks of pool since it's normally pretty quiet in the middle of the night. As I got closer though, I made out a large group of dark shadowy figures drinking pretty hard and pushing each other around. Their voices were muffled and I couldn't make out anything they said, but from what I could see, they looked like the gutter punks that have invaded the city with their piercings and tattoos, gray, raggedy clothing and scraggly hair. It didn't look like anything I wanted to get in the middle of so I took a left on Royal Street and passed by. No one even looked in my direction.

I continued up Royal Street headed towards Canal, almost wading through the slowly breathing white fog. The muffled sounds from the R Bar disappeared behind me. Everything was silent and haunted by the deep gloom. All I could make out were the dark gray shadows of the buildings I passed by. Normally you would hear the tourists still partying on Bourbon Street but that night I couldn't hear a thing. I could barely make out the street sign for St. Phillip Street where I took a right to stop by Lafitte's Blacksmith Shop.

Lafitte's is one of the oldest joints in New Orleans. It was originally built by the legendary pirate Jean Lafitte as a fake blacksmith shop. Lafitte would fence the goods he had stolen from the British cargo ships there. The directions to Lafitte's have always been, walk down Bourbon Street until you come to a building that's falling down and go inside. You found Lafitte's.

My friend Snake played piano at Lafitte's regular so I would usually stop by to see him and swap stories. When I got close to Bourbon and St. Phillip I couldn't hear the piano so I figured Snake finished up early. I stepped inside the front door and the place was full of the same shadowy characters I had seen back at the R Bar. They were murmuring amongst themselves but no one even looked at me. I felt like they didn't know I was there. I looked for Sandy, the regular Friday night bartender, but she wasn't there. In fact, I didn't see any bartenders and I didn't recognize any of the crusty guys in the bar. I walked through the crowd past the tiny burning fireplace that was supposed to have been a forge for blacksmith work to the back door. It suddenly hit me that these guys were speaking in French to each other. I'd taken just enough French in high school to recognize the language. I tried to make eye contact with some of them but they just ignored me, as though they didn't even see me. They spooked me out, so I kept on moving out the back door.

I started swimming through the fog again heading up Bourbon Street towards Canal. Something was creepy because normally there was still some action on Bourbon at this hour of the morning. I guessed the fog had kept the tourists out of the Quarter. The fog was so wet it had begun to soak through my clothes. I put my head down and plowed ahead past Toulouse and St. Louis Streets.

I heard a fog horn sound in the distance, a low moan that vibrated through the street and up my legs. I felt it in my stomach. It was a note so low it couldn't have had a name, followed by another moan that seemed even lower and longer than the first. The third time it growled from even lower and moved up to the same pitched moan as the first two but held on longer before dropping back down again in a slow, dragging fade that finally disappeared. I didn't hear it end as much as I realized it wasn't there anymore.

I had just crossed Bienville Street when I heard a commotion from up ahead of me. Lights glowed dimly in the distance through the slowly breathing fog. I got close to what used to be the Old Absinthe House before it was sold and turned into a flashy daiquiri bar the tourists love.

The Old Absinthe House dated back to 1801 and was where the use of Absinthe in drinks was first started. Back then it was a favorite coffee house and bar for sailors and pirates while they were ashore. It had been one of Lafitte's favorite haunts. The sailors and pirates nailed their cash, left over from booze and whores, to the walls before setting sail and it would be there waiting for them when they returned.

When I got close enough that I could make it out through the lakes of fog, I realized that it was the Old Absinthe House again. The commotion came from drunken pirates smashing their mugs and glasses against the walls and stumbling out the doors. They looked like the same grizzly pirates I had seen back at the R Bar and Lafitte's. The tables were covered with bottles and the stools had been tossed everywhere. Broken glass covered the floor. Candles and kerosene lamps lit the room. I looked inside the Old Absinthe House and the flashing lights and daiquiri machines were gone. The walls were covered with wads of money and notes scratched out on old brown paper. I turned to follow the crowd down Iberville Street and their numbers had swarmed as they met other groups that staggered down Decatur Street.

They were headed towards the river, cursing and shouting in what sounded again like French. I followed them down Bienville to Canal Street where they all headed left towards the Ferry docks. As I got closer, I couldn't see the ferries that were usually tied up there. Instead, through the fog, I made out three huge schooners, each with three masts disappearing up into the fog with great gray sheets of sails flapping in the foggy breeze. There were lines of dinghy's full of the shadowy figures rowing out towards the three ships. There were shouts going back and forth but I couldn't understand the words. It was some other language again.

One dingy was still tied at the dock and a tall thin guy was actually looking towards me and waving me over. I hesitantly started walking towards him until I recognized that cowboy hat, faded tie dyed shirt and snake skin boots. It was Coco smiling back at me. We hugged and slapped. Then he started moving toward the waiting dingy. He turned to look back at me and before I knew I had said it, the same old words fell out of my mouth like so many times before.

"You good, Coco?" I asked.

He smiled and just like he always did, said, "Man, I told you it's all good, didn't I?"

Then Coco turned and walked over to the dingy. He climbed in and followed the others out to the tall, shadowy ships. I watched at the dock as the three schooners turned into the wind that had blown the river fog over the French Quarter. I could just make out Coco waving to me.

The wind shifted and was coming from my back, filling the sails and pushing the schooners downriver. The river fog was blowing off and the sky had lightened to a faint violet. It was 6 AM and the sunrise had just begun to crack the horizon with a line of blood red orange. It burned off the remaining fog and shimmered red, orange and gold across the river. The sun broke through the horizon and sent a blinding glare across the Mississippi, hitting me in the face like a spot light. I pulled my hands out of my pockets and realized I had a bracelet on my left wrist I had never seen before, made out of seashells and wood beads and leather.

I blocked the sunlight with my hands and squinted hard downriver but there was nothing there. Just a light breeze carrying that gravelly voice whispering, "It's all good."

FLYING AWAY WITH MISS COLEEN

by Carolyn Perry

On Saturdays, the French Quarter comes alive mid-morning. One September Saturday, I leave my house, lock my gate, and head toward an 11:15 hair appointment with Charles, a stylist in a salon deep in the bowels of a hotel on St. Louis Street. Wandering tourists amble past me on Royal Street, some looking greenish after a long night of reveling, others already carrying morning go-cups of Bloody Marys or green plastic containers of the fruity but lethal rum drink called a Hand Grenade.

Where Royal intersects St. Louis, a crowd is gathering. The beat of a brass band gets louder as I work my way toward the front. Eight musicians in traditional white shirts, black pants, and caps identifying them as the Pin Stripe Brass Band stroll down St. Louis, horns in the air, their gold plaid ties blown askew and fluttering in the breeze. A trumpet, two trombones, a saxophone, tuba, bass drum and snare drum are belting out the strains of "I'll Fly Away" in the slow cadence of a dirge. A large crowd trails behind at a slow pace, some people holding fringed umbrellas, moving in step to the music—the "second line" of a traditional jazz funeral.

Instead of a casket, three men and a woman push a metal grocery cart decorated with purple, green, and gold feather boas and draped with Mardi Gras beads. These four and scattered others wear gold tee shirts with KREWE OF COLEEN across the front. Behind the cart, two marchers carry a placard on sticks, raised above the heads of the crowd, displaying a large photo of a jolly-looking woman sporting a yellow toque hat with a big red flower.

I crane my neck to see the procession as the band suddenly quickens its pace and breaks into an upbeat version of "Just a Closer Walk with Thee." The crowd quickens too, swaying with the music. They've reached the moment in a jazz funeral called "cutting the body loose." Mourners wave white handkerchiefs, and some begin to dance. A few are in costume: one woman is dressed as a long-whiskered cat, another wears an elaborate Carmen Miranda turban, dripping with cascades of cherries, grapes, and bananas. A few men in coats and ties weave among the tee shirts. It takes several minutes for the procession to move down St. Louis, pass the hotel, and turn onto Chartres Street.

I join the tail end of the second line, behind straggling, curious tourists, some aiming video cameras, and finally I reach the hotel doorway. When I make my way through the lobby and into the salon, Charles is just finishing a client and gives me a wave. This salon's atmosphere is always low-key—it's New Orleans, after all—but on Saturdays there's often a cast of constantly changing characters. A haircut can be an event.

Soon I sit shrouded in a black smock as Charles works his scissors and chats about his adventures during a recent hurricane evacuation.

"I got out early, before the crowds. My neighbor was stuck on the highway in Mississippi for *five hours*—gawd. Says next time she's not going." New Orleans had emptied in fear of Gustav, but this time the storm skirted the city.

A piercing cackle arises from a chair across the room where Warren, another stylist, is waving a blow dryer around the head of a middle-aged woman he's given a pixie cut. Her two friends stand near, gazing at themselves in mirrors that line the wall, talking about a "paw-ty" and hung-over husbands. They wear tight pants and shirts tied at the midriff, and their necks and shoulders are draped with multiple strands of plastic Mardi Gras beads bearing the logo of a nearby casino. One pours liberally from a champagne bottle, and raucous laughter follows every comment. Warren observes their antics, an indulgent smile on his face.

Sotto voce, Charles says to me, "That's the wife of a bigwig from Mississippi. They're getting ready for what they call a Mardi Gras party. Fools, it's September."

"The party's started early," I say, as one of the ladies dances around the manicure chairs, humming "Mardi Gras Mambo" and waving a flute of champagne. Another fills two more glasses and brings them over to Charles and me.

"Can't do it," says Charles. "I might start cutting zig zag hair. Thanks anyway."

"Cheers," I say, accepting the glass of frothy bubbles and taking a sip.

In the door breezes a younger woman with long red hair.

"Hi, y'all!" To Charles she says, "I know I'm early, baby, but I'm here."

"Nice shirt," calls Warren from across the room. All heads swivel toward the newcomer. She pulls her shoulders back, displaying an ample bosom beneath a black tee shirt emblazoned with GO GO BOYS in glittering rhinestones.

"Don'tcha love it? I found it at Saks—Gucci marked down and down and down. I said, I gotta buy that and wear it to the salon."

"Fabulous," says Charles. "Definitely you."

"Miss Coleen is having a huge party down the street, y'all," says Redhead. "Big band, great music, lots of drinks, lots of folks. I passed by, almost stopped."

Mambo Lady dances over and presses a flute of champagne into Redhead's hand. She smiles.

"Ooooh, Bubbly—just what I need."

"Miss Coleen?" says Charles. "On Chartres?"

"Yeah, 900 block. That author. I don't know her name—I've always just called her Miss Coleen."

"She passed," says Charles.

"What? What you mean passed? She's having a party."

"Died Tuesday," says Charles. "Her funeral's today."

"Well, it's definitely a party."

Hearing the name Coleen and the word *author*, all at once I'm back, seated at a round table for eight during one of the Hotel Monteleone's literary luncheons the previous year. The four other women and two men at the table had introduced themselves to one another and were making conversation while they sipped their drinks. We were an assortment of teachers, writers, a director of a literacy program, and friends of the day's speaker. A waiter stepped up and took away the chair from the empty place setting to my right, and into it rolled a rotund woman steering a motorized chair. She had large red-framed glasses, long grey hair pulled back in a bun, a wide smile, and jiggly jowls.

"Good afternoon," she said in a thick Southern drawl. "How's everybody?" Faces lit up at her arrival, and she greeted most people at the table by name. They seemed to know her well.

"I've got another grandchild in love with your books, Coleen," said one woman. "All three of mine always ask for the possum first."

"Epossumondas. That's nice to hear. I'll have another one out soon." As the waiter served her drink, she turned to me, obviously the only one at the table unknown to her, and said, "I'm Coleen Salley. I write books for children, and I love to tell stories."

I introduced myself and we chatted about her books, and about living in the French Quarter. Ms. Salley had a warm manner and a delightfully expressive voice. It was easy to picture her with a gaggle of rapt children sitting at her feet, hanging on every word. Later, I learned that was exactly how she spent a lot of her life. After a long career as an award-winning teacher at the University of New Orleans and visiting professor at other colleges, she retired as UNO Distinguished

Professor of Children's Literature. At the age of 72, Coleen Salley published the first of her own books, an adaptation of the "Three Billy Goats Gruff" tale set in Louisiana, titled *Who's That Tripping Over My Bridge?* She soon became known for her re-creations of Southern folktales in a series featuring a charming possum called Epossumondas. She was in demand at schools and libraries all over the country.

After meeting her, I looked for Coleen Salley's books and learned she was a genuine French Quarter character. Her house on Chartres Street was a regular stop on Christmas home tours, highlighted by seven different Christmas trees she always decorated with souvenirs from her travels. From 1974 on, she reigned over her own Mardi Gras walking parade, the Krewe of Coleen. On Fat Tuesday they pushed their queen, riding in her decorated grocery buggy, all over the Quarter.

Almost a year passed before I saw the name Coleen Salley again, this time in a *Times-Picayune* obituary. Ms. Salley died on September 16, 2008, in Baton Rouge, having evacuated for Hurricane Gustav. A celebration of her life was planned for September 26. Two years later, friends, former students, and family would install a statue of two characters from Coleen Salley's books: Mama and Epossumondas. Mama wears the familiar yellow toque with the red flower and looks exactly like the author herself, and she holds a diapered Epossumondas on her lap. Miss Coleen's beloved characters now sit permanently on a bench in Story Land in New Orleans' City Park, where they continue to delight visiting young readers.

After leaving the salon that Saturday in September with my new haircut, I walk down Chartres Street and hear distant horns blaring out "When the Saints Go Marching In." As I pass St. Louis Cathedral and Jackson Square, the music swells. Two blocks farther downriver, people I'd seen marching earlier are crowding the sidewalk, spilling out of a doorway, drinking champagne from plastic flutes, swaying to the exuberant music. The feathered, beaded grocery cart sits in front of the door, the placard with the smiling photo propped above it. When the band reaches a flourishing finish to "Saints," one gold-tee-shirted man shakes a tambourine and calls for a toast. The crowd gathers close around the cart.

"H-a-i-l!" shouts the leader, and people in the circle raise glasses then bow low from the waist or curtsey in the street. "The *Q-u-e-e-n!*" The shout is repeated twice, and each time the mourners hold glasses high, sip their champagne, and bow, sweeping handkerchiefs along the ground in homage to the deceased, who reigned as Queen of the Krewe of Coleen and whose ashes reside in the brass urn resting beneath her picture in the grocery cart—her Mardi Gras chariot.

After the toast, the band strikes up "Basin Street Blues," the mourners replenish their glasses, and this being New Orleans, the party goes on.

ALAN

by Jason Affolder

My friend Alan was a real nice guy, but living in New Orleans nearly ruined him. The incessant drinking and carousing we engaged in rotted his brain and regularly turned him into a cartoonish wild man he was not comfortable playing. Finally he realized it would be the end of him and fled NOLA like a sinking ship after less than a year. This is one of the last misadventures we shared...

That night we sat in Bangkok Thai Restaurant, next to Cooter Brown's Tavern, finishing some spicy grub of the Asian persuasion. We had arrived already drunk, and the heat of the cuisine only accelerated our intake of beer. During the process of eating Alan had spilled food down his front, and when the waitress arrived to inquire if we needed anything else, he suddenly ripped his soiled shirt off and tossed it on the table.

"You can take that away," Alan slurred, then stumbled toward the exit as he lit up a cigarette, leaving me to handle the bill and the apology. As I paid I tried to keep an eye on him through the glass front door but he soon disappeared from view. Once our debt was settled I rushed outside to search for him.

The spring night was cool and everyone had a jacket or at least a shirt on, so spotting Alan shouldn't have been difficult, but there were no bare-chested drunks visible in any direction. I walked toward the levee, hoping he hadn't set out to go swimming in the Mississippi again, when I heard an angry voice yell, "GET THE FUCK OUTTA HERE!" and saw my friend flung from the front door of Cooter Brown's, lit cigarette still dangling from his mouth and fresh bottle of beer in hand. He struggled to stay upright as he awkwardly danced across the sidewalk, Budweiser sloshing out onto his arm, then finally regained his balance. After taking a deep drag from his smoke, he threw his head back and sucked down the remaining beer before smashing the bottle on the sidewalk in an explosion of glass and sprinting off manically. I chased after him but he was always a fast fucker, faster still running on alcohol.

Turning the corner I saw Alan far ahead and called out his name, but this only made him more determined to lose me. He soon passed a motorcycle parked on the sidewalk and slowed down to knock it over as an obstacle for me, the loud crash of metal on concrete making lights in a nearby house flick on. Seeing Alan continue on his original trajectory, I made a quick turn to circle the block and avoid meeting the fallen bike's certainly angry owner. I now reckoned my friend was heading back to our house and hoped to head him off in Audubon Park, but when I reached the wide, empty expanse of open golf course there he was nowhere to be seen. I started off across the rolling terrain, a shortcut home, when my guts suddenly started growling fiercely. I knew something had to be done, and quickly, so locating the closest green, I squatted over the hole there and emptied my bowels into it for some unlucky golfer to find the next day. With little hesitation I scurried onward, not wishing to explain myself to the park security guards.

Eventually I reached the shotgun house Alan and I shared on Webster Street and realized he had the only key left, the rest having been lost in various other drunken escapades of late. I checked the door, just in case Alan had actually made it home, but it was locked tight, so I laid down on the porch and passed out waiting for him to return.

Hours later my eyes crept open to realize it was nearly dawn, the sky brightening up quickly as I rolled over and groaned at the pains in my skull and spine. Sitting on my butt and resting my aching head on my knees, I heard someone approaching and glanced over to see Alan walking down the sidewalk. He had a small bundle of cloth held gingerly in his hand, which he threw in our trash can as he passed through the wrought iron gate. He looked melancholy.

"What is that, man? You okay?" I asked.

Alan spoke to me glumly as he climbed the front steps and dug the house key out of his pocket. "I shit my pants."

"Oh man, that sucks. Almost happened to me too. I had to crap out on the golf course. Thai food."

Alan shook his head. "No, I did it on purpose. I stopped on the running track in the park and squatted down and just squeezed it out into my underwear."

I waited a second in confusion before inquiring, "Why?"

Alan shrugged. "I wanted to see if I could still do it. It should be easy, I mean babies can do it... But it was pretty hard."

With that Alan unlocked the front door and entered the house. Lifting the lid off the garbage can I did indeed see a pair of poop-filled boxers resting inside. After a moment of contemplation I replaced the cover and followed my friend inside.

Less than a month later Alan departed New Orleans and never looked back, went and made something of himself as an internationally renowned artist. He doesn't talk to me much anymore. But I will always remember that night when he tore his shirt off and shit his pants.

MADELINE
by Jason Affolder

It only took two hurricanes and a bottle of Wild Turkey
to finally get us together.

To elaborate:
Katrina had knocked out the city,
Rita had kicked it while it was down.
Only now, over a month after the fight began,
were vital signs returning to New Orleans.
This was the setting for our fling...

Madeline and I had skirted the edge of romance for nearly a year, ever since we met in that ashtray of a bar known as Brothers 3 and stayed up drinking cheap whiskey until dawn, when duty at the firehouse called me away. In the meantime I was still engaged in a dying relationship, refusing infidelity partly out of principle but mostly because I was gutless. At last that predicament had been mercifully euthanized by the same storms which had shattered levees and leveled houses. In fact, the destruction of New Orleans was possibly the best thing that had ever happened to me: My ex was far away and forever departed from my life, my domicile was intact, spared by the wind and the water, plenty of hurricane hazard pay flowed into my coffers... And now Madeline was returning, if only for a weekend.

She arrived on one of the first flights to allow civilians on board and caught a ride into the city with a friend who was military, could easily pass through blockades at the parish line. When this girl actually appeared in my quiet, empty, powerless neighborhood that afternoon it had an overwhelming sense of surreality, but our reunion began with a simple platonic hug and a bit of informal catching up: She had relocated to Maine before the storm's arrival and only a few phone calls had kept us in touch since then. While we spoke of things large and small I felt that old turbulence creeping along my spine and unceremoniously cracked open a virgin bottle of Wild Turkey... Not the pussified 80 proof shit that amateurs and cowards drink. Wild Turkey 101. 50% alcohol. 0% mercy. Hard to come by in these disastrous times, I had received it from a bartender at the Balcony Bar in gratitude for helping to save his house from a fire that reduced the rest of the block to ashes.

So without hesitation we began tossing back slugs of whiskey straight from the bottle, the first shots sizzling down our throats, grimacing our faces, and loosening our tensions. Hunger took hold quickly and we prepared a dinner of MREs, filling the water-activated heating pouches with precious Turkey to warm up the military entrees. I had the burrito, she the cannelloni, the over-processed soldier food going down fast and filling our empty stomachs well as we watched the sun dying from my front porch, its glory intensified by the growing bourbon buzz in our heads.

This sedentary boozing continued while the sky bruised and slowly painted black. These were dark times, literally, with generators providing artificial light in just a few scattered windows, so it was by the faint illumination falling from naked stars and a sliver of moon that we set out to wander the city's abandoned streets on foot. Curfew was in effect, demanding the inhabitants of this almost-ghost town remain inside at night "to prevent looting and other crimes." This meant every time we saw the blinding beams of a National Guard patrol approaching, Madeline and I were forced to scurry between houses or dive behind a dumpster to hide while military vehicles crept past with searchlights sweeping. It felt like we were on the run from Nazis in occupied France, a supremely romantic notion, but still I was too terrified to break the invisible barrier lingering between us. Instead we were driven farther and farther away from my neighborhood by our unwitting pursuers, the contents of the bottle in my hand continuing its flow into our stomachs one chug at a time.

After an hour of this cat-and-mousery with the soldiers we inadvertently arrived at the lonely Prytania movie theatre, its normally welcoming facade asleep with every other business along the street. Suddenly realizing there was enough liquid courage in my veins to act, I set down the half-empty bottle of Turkey in the middle of the street and gracefully grabbed Madeline by the waist to pull her close. Without hesitation our mouths met and months of longing and frustration evaporated in one desperate, fluid kiss. Stumbling together, we collapsed onto the front steps of the theatre, where we had each stood waiting in line for tickets countless times apart but never together. Writhing on the gritty bricks, lips and hands explored foreign territory until the growl of another prowling Humvee rudely interrupted. We startled to our feet as it cruised closer and synchronously bolted toward deeper shadows, me sweeping the bottle of whiskey back into my grip as we ran hand-in-hand.

Hearts thundering in our chests, more bourbon than blood in our veins, we finally reached the safety of my home and instantly resumed our animal groping. As clothes came off the suffocating heat of this late September night pressed in on us, so I swept open the front door to welcome any trace of humid breeze inside. The darkness within the house was complete, everything revealed by touch or taste. Time stretched out and was forgotten.

Once the things we were doing were done, we lay naked and sweating on the hardwood floor, chasing breath and swatting mosquitoes off one another. The pulse in my ears still roared so loudly I didn't notice the engine outside until a violent spotlight blasted through the front door, etching our naked forms in stark whiteness. The soldiers behind the brilliance demanded we identify ourselves as I reached for a sheet to cover Madeline, a pair of pants for myself. Driver's license and fire department credentials proved to the inquisitors that I belonged here, and so with a sleazy wink the guardsmen resumed their meandering search. Madeline and I laughed heartily and without embarrassment at the situation while drinking down the last dregs of Wild Turkey. Eventually unconsciousness took over our entangled bodies and the empty whiskey bottle rolled across the floor, hiding under a couch for me to discover months later.

The days following were a similar blur of drink, talk, sex, laughter. Finally Madeline returned to New England, where she now belonged, just as the fire department called me back to duty. We went about our separate lives and casually, painlessly drifted apart; we both knew a normal relationship would never compare to the brief intensity with which we had burned. It was a strange tryst that could only have existed the moment that it did, while reality lay unraveled and the whiskey made us both honest and fearless, if only for a hiccup of time.

Excerpts from HACK

by Leonard Lopp

VEHICULAR PROSTITUTE

5/27/09 Wed. 61.6 miles

After waiting thirty minutes at the Pontchartrain cab stand I was dispatched to an address in the Lower Garden District. There are nine streets in this area named after the Muses in Greek mythology. I picked up my fare on Melpomene, the Muse of Tragedy, which seemed all too fitting. She was a thirty-something woman who was drunk as hell. I'm talking cartoon style drunk. She hiccuped her address to me and we were on our way towards Esplanade Avenue.

"Wait. Can you take me to McDonald's," she giggled.

"Sure, which one do you want to go to?" There was a long pause, then she just repeated her address. I rolled my eyes and proceeded to the original destination. She tried her best to have a conversation but she hiccuped every time she tried to say anything. After a few minutes of her hiccuping to me she began to giggle.

"How long have you been driving a cab?" Before I could even answer she cut me off. "Hey, white boy! Hey, white boy! What you doin' drivin a cab?" She laughed, then giggled for a solid minute, then hiccuped again. "Can you take me to McDonald's?"

As I pulled into the drive thru she asked, "What do you want papi? I'm gonna feed you real good."

"Oh, I'm full. I already ate. Thanks," I replied.

"I'm gonna order so much food you won't know what to eat first!"

"No, really. I don't want anything."

"Oh c'mon, I know you're hungry. What? You don't eat this kinda stuff?"

"Oh, Lord." I sighed, exhausted by her drunkenness.

"Where do you want to go?" She asked.

This went on for minutes as we sat in the drive thru. All of the lights in the place were on but nobody ever came to the drive thru window. She sat up on the front part of the back-seat, reached over my seat and started rubbing my shoulders. She then told me again, in what might have been her sexy voice, how well she was going to feed me. I leaned forward and pretended to look into the drive thru window.

"I don't think anyone's coming," I said. "There's a Rally's right there. Is that cool?"

I pulled up the drive thru lane as she climbed halfway out the rear window.

"Welcome to Rally's. Can I take your order?"

"Yeah, gimme... three triple cheeseburgers," she screamed at the speaker box.

I pulled the Lincoln up so that the rear window was even with the drive thru window.

"That'll be $10.87 Ma'am."

She fumbled through her purse for a few seconds then cursed. The drive thru guy looked at me. I gave a half smile and shook my head. He flashed the same knowing smile. Both of us had obviously dealt with too many drunk people in our lives.

"Shit, I don't have enough money. Papi give me five bucks," she demanded.

"What? Yeah right. Why you ordering three triple cheese-burgers if you got no money?" I asked.

The drive thru guy pulled two of the artery clogging burgers out of the bag and sold the lady one instead.

"I hope you got a credit card." I told her. As I pulled out of the drive thru she threw the triple cheeseburger in the front seat. "There you go papi!"

"I told you baby, I'm not hungry." I repeated.

"Oh. What? Now you don't want it?" She said. "Fine! I'll eat it!"

She reached over the seat, grabbed the bag then fell into the backseat. Sitting directly in the middle of the backseat she ripped open the bag, unwrapped the burger, and propped her right leg on the armrest of the passenger door. She devoured about half of it with one bite.

So there she was with a mouthful of triple cheeseburger sitting spread eagle in my backseat.

"Do you wanna take me?"

I was trying so hard not to laugh that I, literally, bit my tongue.

"What, you didn't understand me?" She demanded.

"Lady, I haven't understood much of anything since you got in the car."

"Fine," she murmured and took another bite of her triple cheeseburger. "I wanna hang out with you. Can I buy you a drink?" she said as she wolfed down the last bit of the burger.

"Lady, I'm working right now and I drive for a living. I can't really be having drinks." I replied.

"Oh, c'mon... you can leave the meter on, papi."

I just let that statement hang in the air.

"Oh, fine. Whatever! My old man would find out and probably kill me anyway."

My friend Peter refers to me as a vehicular prostitute. He says, "You'll let anyone into your car as long as they pay you."

Tonight... I definitely felt like one tonight.

THE DRUNK PROFESSOR & HIS CHICKEN

09/27/09 Sun. 90.8 miles
09/28/09 Mon. 51.2 miles
09/29/09 Tues. 84.6 miles
09/30/09 Wed. 57.5 miles
10/01/09 Thurs. 74.6 miles

September was the promise from the older cabbies and all the dispatchers. That's when business will pick up and I will no longer have to work seven days a week to make ends meet. I'm not the only one either. I hear the same cab numbers everyday. That means there's a bunch of us working seven days a week. Well, today is October 1st and the "ends aren't meeting." In fact, they aren't even close. It's 9:00 PM on a Thursday night and I sit fourth out at Touro. I've been running errands all day looking for a chance to jump in and make a few bucks but the stands have been full all day.

There are barely any cabs available to rent in my company right now. That means we have more cabs than ever on the road (421 to be exact) and less business. The conventions have started back up but even that business is slow. I'm beginning to feel like there is always a carrot being dangled in front of me. This weekend, next week, next month, you won't be such a poor bastard.

It was twenty-two minutes before I finally got an order from the Touro Stand. It was for the Balcony Bar.

"I'm going to the Lakefront," he said opening the back door.

"As in Lakeview… Lakefront?" I asked.

"Yeah, is that OK?" He asked. I wasn't exactly thrilled.

"Of course, man. I'll take you anywhere you want to go," I told him.

He got in and immediately asked if he could smoke a cigarette. I'm always astonished how people can't wait twenty minutes to smoke a god damn cigarette. I agreed knowing it would pay off in the end. It was a beautiful night out and I had the windows rolled down anyway.

The conversation veered very little from the standard questions a cabbie is normally faced with. He told me he had just moved back to New Orleans from California after ten years, but for some reason I didn't believe him. I felt like I had seen him around before. I felt like he had made a bad impression on me during my disgruntled bartender years. What did I care anyway. He was putting me on and I was, in ways, putting him on. At times I get so bored of answering the same questions over and over that I stretch the truth. Sometimes I tell people about the "Hack" project, sometimes I don't. I always make sure to tell them that I have higher artistic aspirations though. It usually equals a bigger tip in the end. People, especially tourists, like to think they've ridden with a crazy New Orleanian or a talented young artist who is biding his time until the break comes. Sometimes, like in this situation, I tell people I'm a busker in the French Quarter playing guitar with my hands and drums with my feet.

We finally arrived at his house thirty minutes later after stopping at a gas station so he could buy beer. He kept saying the whole time that he would make it "worth my while" but I seldom believe people when they tell me such things. He held true to his word and dropped $60 on a $27 fare. I was shocked.

"Yo man, you can't give me this much," I told him.

"Don't worry, man. Just play your music," he said.

"You're crazy," I repeated.

"Play your music, man," he repeated and closed the door.

Thank goodness for that fare. Without it I would have made no money at all tonight. I had 4 No Loads tonight. One of which, I'm sure, was taken by a cabbie from my company. It's been so slow that even our own guys are stealing from each other constantly.

Around 2:00 AM I was sent to an address on St. Charles. I honked my horn and waited five minutes but no one came out. I turned around on St. Charles and took a left up the side street that bordered the huge mansion. I pulled up to the side of the house and saw an older pudgy guy standing outside. He quickly ran inside and started screaming something. A minute later he came out shaking his head.

"Listen, I'm really sorry. I'm trying to get her to leave but she refuses," he said. I could hear a woman bitching inside the house. He pulled out a wad of singles and handed them to me. "This is for your time," he said and shuffled back inside. It's very rare for someone to be so considerate. I wondered what the hell that guy had gotten himself into.

I decided it was time to park the cab and grab a drink. I stopped by a gas station to get a snack. I sat in the parking lot eating nacho chips topped with hot orange cheese product. An American Cab Company cab driver pulled up behind me honking his horn. I ignored him and continued with my snack. I was woken from my cheese product haze by a rapping on my passenger window.

There stood three young college kids and one older guy, who was holding two bags of Brother's Fried Chicken.

"That guy said you would take us to the College," the older guy said. I was completely confused, munching on my nachos and looking at them with skepticism.

"Your telling me that… that cab driver, my competitor, put you out of his cab and told you to ride with me?"

"Yeah," they agreed in unison.

"Why?" I questioned.

"He just said you'd take us," the older guy said.

"I find it hard to believe. Why'd he put you out? Did you guys get into a fight?

"No," they responded.

"Where you giving him a hard time?"

"No," they responded.

"Did one of you vomit in his cab?"

"No, No. Listen man. I want you to drive these kids back to Tulane then drive me back here," the older guy said.

"Here? Back to this gas station?" I asked chewing on another nacho.

"Well, Prytania," he said.

"Do you have money?" I asked.

"Yes," he said frustratingly flapping his bags of chicken. "I'm a Tulane professor for Christ sake!"

"OK, let's go. You can't blame me for questioning though. It seems a little fishy that that guy would put you out for no reason," I said. They all agreed.

The ride to Tulane was nothing short of ridiculous. The older guy was bombed to the point that his eyes were rolling into the back of his head. He talked absolute nonsense the whole time. Then, he wanted me to take him to a store to buy more beer.

"Yeah, that's a great idea. I think that's exactly what you need," said the girl from the back seat.

"Man, it's three in the morning and you don't want to be stopping at any place around here to buy booze," I told him. "There are a few bars on the way though."

The girl in the backseat leaned forward and whispered into my left ear, "Please, just take us back to the Tulane." We arrived shortly there after and the three kids quickly jumped out the back seat. One of the guys handed the drunk professor five dollars for their share of the cab ride.

"Be sure to take my class next semester," he slurred.

"Yeah! Right," the girl said walking away from the cab.

"They jus' don' get it," the professor said.

"Of course they don't. They're young. I'm sure you were just as clueless as they are when you were a kid. I know I was," I replied.

"Yeah, you right. But they won' eva get it. Ther' these rich bastard kids from the East Coast. They don' understand shit," he slurred.

"Sure, maybe they won't. But most people don't understand anything outside of themselves. Whether rich or poor," I replied. There was a long pause as we pulled up to Prytania a few blocks from where he lived.

"Are you gay?" He asked with glassy lustful eyes.

"No, sorry." I replied.

"Well, you're the mos' nderstanding straight guy I've ever met," he said as we pulled up to the address he told me. He gave me a twenty dollar bill and clumsily climbed out of the car. He crossed the street and continued walking well past the address he gave me. I looked over at the passenger seat and saw the five dollar bill the one kid had given to the professor sitting crumpled on the seat. Bonus! In my side mirror I watched the professor walk into the darkness carrying two bags of fried chicken.

SETTLING WATER

by Rex Dinger

"What cruel things the sea can do to the mind," he started. I nodded in agreement to the young, weather beaten man sitting next to me, not knowing exactly what he was talking about or where he was going with it. I, myself, know nothing of the sea or its effects on the mind. Ordinarily I would ignore such barroom chatter, but sometimes a person needs to be heard.

"You see," he began abruptly, "I'd been at sea for just under a year and twice I'd almost lost my head." I nodded politely, again, and responded with a grunt typical of a man's show of interest in a story. "There are times when all you have to do is think, to stare out at the endless water and think. Some might say that thinking is a good thing, but not when it is all you have to do. The mind needs diversion every now and then. When all you have to do is think, your mind goes from bad to worse, the thoughts grow more evil as they run and twist into dark corridors and take away your last vestiges of sanity."

He let out a sigh and smirked as though he remembered an old acquaintance he was fond of. I wondered how long it would be before he lost his mind and would begin bludgeoning me with his barstool or the nearest blunt object. The people in the bar would just stare in disbelief, not knowing if they were seeing something real. Some of them would rub their eyes, others would scream. Still, you never know about these people that have something to say. One can never be too careful. I was curious, though, what all he had gone through, what terrible thoughts he had manifested, what he had been before he had become this disillusioned creature.

"People will always say they love the sea, that it's so calming and easy to relax by. But when you live there, when you have that serenity always about you, it becomes monotony, it becomes as crazed as any city. Once you realize you've been broken by the sea, that's when the madness sets in." He paused, looked down at his beer, now nothing more than a last warm swallow, and drank it. "That's when the madness sets in."

I thought of buying him another beer because sometimes heavy-hearted people need someone to buy them a beer. I decided against it, fearing it may be interpreted as a sign of companionship that would ultimately solicit a whole life's story instead of a time passed. He relieved me of the burden by gesturing to the bartender, who responded with a move to the tap with an empty glass. He stared forward so I did the same, as though we were strangers that had never spoken. I wanted to look over, to analyze the face for tragedy, but I didn't. I didn't because it might bring more of a story I was not certain whether or not I wanted to hear.

"You don't recognize the lunacy because it is slow made," he said without my prodding. Now I looked over, realizing I would hear what he had to say one way or the other. "You can't see it until it is upon you, covering you like an invisible vine, entwining its madness around you, through you. Then it becomes you and there is no difference between you and it and you're stripped from the you you once were. Nothing is left but crazed eyes and a quick tongue. Your heart moves like a serpent, winding into evil apple trees beckoning all innocents near to eat your forbidden fruit.

"Even the sanest of people go mad. I found myself thinking at times of different ways to bomb the ship, or whacking some foreigner in the head with a hammer, or jumping overboard and feed myself to the sharks. I never did any of these things, though. Somehow I was always able to bring myself back to the grey world of sanity."

Here is the violence, I thought, here is the dark side of this man that is lying dormant, waiting around to "whack" me in the head with something. I made no move to suggest an assault, lest it be misinterpreted and the serpent he spoke of reveal its ugly head. I was trapped, entwined into the tale whether or not I wanted to be. I would listen now for my own survival.

"Do you know what I did to finally keep myself a little on the sane side?" He looked over and finally made eye contact with me. For sure I was trapped now. I lifted my eyebrows while curling the sides of my mouth downward to imply that I was vaguely curious as to what it could be.

"Well, let me tell you," he continued, as I knew he would, "I would keep a tray of grass in my room. A legitimate tray of grass. We were in a port in some dingy Mexican town and I found myself lying on the grass watching the sunset one evening. Just sprawled out in the grass like a dog, a beaten dog. It was a helluva day, helluva day and I was sure to be bound for the nut house that day. I spent the first half of my day painting and crying. I'm not ashamed to say I cry like most men now that I've had something to cry about.

"Just like pops used to say, 'I'll give you somethin' to cry about you little nigger. You'll know pain when I'm through whipping your ass until you bleed.' He wasn't a smart man, but he loved us all in between the drinking spells. Anyway, there I was in Mexico, in a grimy port town, in this little spot of Heaven. It's not many ports that have tufts of grass lying about. And there I was, staring up at the sunset, taking in the whole scene and loving it.

"I realized that I was pulling the blades of grass and throwing them above me, throwing them into the light wind that was blowing. I knew that when I got up I'd be all itchy, but for a moment it was absolute bliss, for a moment it was all the happy memories and still moments when reality slips away in a good way and you are at peace with the world. The tiny blades reaching through my clothes giving me tiny pricks on my back, oh, it was like I was a kid again.

"It's one of those pleasures that we have all taken for granted, like the crunch of snow under your boots or the way sand shapes itself between your toes at the beach. People never stop to think of what a pleasure it is to sit in the grass, they always expect it to be there, and then when you don't have it, you can appreciate it. So as homage to my appreciation for grass, I bought a kitty litter tray and filled it with good soil and then laid a square of grass it in.

"Of course, some of them thought I was crazy, but every time I got to missing the true feel of earth, I could take my shoes off and stand firmly on the ground. A small consolation in that prison, but worth all the crap I had to go through to keep it up. I kept it in my favorite corner of the cabin.

"You see, 'coz, there are times when you don't feel like much of a man because they treat you lower than a dog and that can take its toll after a while. You get to believing that you're a piece of shit. And sometimes the only thing that makes you feel like a man again, the only thing that restores the inside of you, is the endless tears you shed on many a lonely night. Men aren't supposed to cry, but they do, they all do when they're hid away, when they've tucked themselves into a tiny corner where no one will see them.

"Of course, you think, oh, that would restore everything alright then, wouldn't it? But that would be too easy, that would be far too easy. Because then, the next day when you got to look at the water again, you begin to think that you're not much of a man for crying because men aren't supposed to cry. But they do. That's why there's no shame in me saying that I've cried because I think I earned it. 'I'll give you something to cry about.'"

He laughed mockingly at himself, or maybe at his good father who had brought him up on opinions of his own.

This time I needed a beer, but thought it was best to maybe use this as my chance to get away. Off to the office, I could say, but there'd be no office. Have to get back home, but that might not be the best thing to say either. It was solved when he lifted his index finger slightly into the air above his beer and then pointed in my direction, indicating to the bartender that he was getting a beer for the thirsty listener.

"The tray of grass was my little piece of sanity. After a long distance fight with my girl, I even bought a few periwinkles to put around the side of the tray so I could stand in the middle. I had my own little garden. I called it my garden of sanity, but as I said, it was no bigger than a kitty litter box."

My beer arrived at the beginning of an uncomfortable silence, allowing me an excuse to not break it, not wanting to. "What made you go crazy?" I heard some voice asking and shocked to discover it was my own. Damnable mouth always speaking out of turn. I should have the god-forsaken tongue cut out one day and I will if it ever really gets me into trouble. I'll walk around a mute, slobbering nonsensical words and people will give me quarters on the street to make me go away.

"The first time it was slow coming, as I said, it's always slow coming. Lunacy spawned from isolation moving like thick molasses. I got on board the ship three days before Mardi Gras and I ain't never missed a Mardi Gras before and we sailed to Rio Haina in the Dominican Republic. We passed the city, it seemed, just as the parade was turning off Canal Street headin' towards the Convention Center. It may have only taken about fifteen or twenty minutes to get passed the heart of New Orleans, but it felt as though it was fifteen or twenty years.

"I been in this relationship with this girl and I liked her, still do now, and, as we passed the French Quarter heading to Algiers Point to make the bend, standing on the deck looking at the city all lit up in night, I thought of every single damned place we'd ever gone. It hurt. I cried a little bit there, but not too much because I didn't want the others to see and think I was a sissy. Men aren't supposed to cry, you know.

"Well, I was the only person on the ship that spoke English. As a first language. Most of them were Spanish speakers or Greek. That right there spells isolation 'cause I didn't speak either, still don't. The whole trip down to this port, Rio Haina, they keep askin' if I'm going into town for puta, that's a whore in Spanish. I'm not because I made a promise and I got a girl, but they don't understand that much because Latino people think it's their right to have a bit on the side.

"We get there a few days later, hang around in an anchorage for a few days more, and then once we get into the port, it's a cesspool. Like nothing you'd ever see here. The city itself is like one exposed sewer, like the canals when they flood and leave the mess all over the road. And all them dirty little monkeys; they all want to be your friend 'cause you're a gringo. That's Spanish for whitey. See they love the American, but they'd no sooner love you than knock you over the head with something to steal your Nikes.

"I had this one guy that wanted to take me to dinner to meet his sister and cousin, both single, in case I'd be interested in one of them. 'They beautiful, okay Joe.' Okay Joe, like a damned Chinese kid in those horrible Vietnam movies. They speak Spanish there, by the way, so I was still at a loss. He was hopin' I'd fall in love with one of his relatives and bring 'em to the home of the free and the land of the brave. Whatever, the point of it is that I didn't have any friends on the ship, didn't know who to trust and was scared shitless of the port just from the looks of it. No one on board ever made a move to be my friend, so I thought they didn't like me.

"I locked myself up in my room at night and just stayed there. Here's the part where I finally went a little loony. We leave this shithouse and head to Trinidad, not much better than there because we were in some industrial place. At least they speak English, right? Anyway, as we sit in anchorage for two or three weeks, we have to begin rationing water 'cause the ship is running low on water; we only get an hour to shower and all else. All that water in the middle of the Caribbean and not a fucking drop on the ship. To beat that, we start running out of food and eat roast and rotten potatoes for eight days straight.

"Now, had I been smart, I wouldn't have left my stereo at home, nor would I have taken out the books that my mother gave me out of my bag. 'Maybe you'll learn to appreciate the readin' when you don't got no English on that ship.' At nights, with no friends, there I was, in my room, alone, more alone than ever before. I had only my thoughts at night and during the day, only the water and the far off land to think about. And my girl, God, I was always waiting for some news that she'd shacked up with some other guy because he was there and I wasn't.

"We worked every day, Sundays and holidays too. Except Christmas. They didn't give me my holidays because they weren't Greek holidays and on Greek holidays when they took off, I didn't get them because I wasn't Greek. The officers were Greek. One Sunday I decide I'm sick of it, sick of the whole damned thing and I don't show up to work. I sleep-in in the morning, wake up for lunch and then the shit hits the fan. Captain's all in my face yelling about not working and I'm yelling back that he can eat shit and I don't work Sundays for what I'm paid. And on and on.

"I end up back in my cell, pissed off, missing home, missing all things American, missing my girl and even missing the English language. Then I break down, sit in my favorite corner, where the grass is now, and begin crying, mumbling to myself that it'll be okay and all that. Well, you'd think I went off my rocker all the way if I told you some of the things I was thinkin', but sometime that night, a good seven hours later, I was able to pull myself out of it. That's really the reason it's my favorite corner.

"There's nowhere to go when you're on a ship in the middle of the sea but overboard to the sharks. To the watery grave. Walk the plank! So you either kill yourself or adjust. I decided to adjust the best that I could. I wasn't much over it until I finally got back home the first time and brought back a radio and some books. Sounds funny, but it's a different kinda prison altogether, different altogether. You know what it's like to be in prison? You ought to go to sea if you want to find out without committin' a crime. Sure enough, you'll get the feel for it. Sure enough."

A blank expression took over his face, reminding me of how my father used to get when he thought about the war. That vacant, desperately pained look that had no real expression to it but in its intensity. Suddenly he gestured to the bartender for two more, but I, noticing the time, changed the order from two to one with a gesture of my own. "Have to get going," I told him, and I really did. I tapped my watch, more my wrist really, to emphasize that I was on a schedule of some sort. He nodded, he understood.

"I'm Mike, by the way," he said with a certain vacuity about him as he stretched out his hand to greet mine.

"I'm Mike too," I responded with an acute sense of autonomy that convinced even myself and turned, leaving him to the cure for his pain.

TWENTY-FIRST CENTURY PEASANT

by J. Michael Hinkhouse

Dirty couch seats and a balsa wood coffee table, which was the foundation for a dirty bowl of dried rice, a half drank plastic cup of tap water, and two unpaid electric bills, sat in the living room that opened up invitingly to Cameron every night after work. Of course there wasn't always two electric bills waiting to be paid and the cup of water might at some points be a flat can of beer or a bag of potato chips with stale crumbs at the bottom, but nonetheless, that is how every night's return home could be remembered. And keeping the variables uncomplicated for you, Reader, we'll just say that every night sat a dirty bowl of dried rice, a half drank plastic cup of tap water, and two unpaid electric bills upon Cameron's balsa wood coffee table. That table, the dirty couch, the corner bookshelf, and his mattress were all acquired from the side of the road.

Cameron flipped on the lights and trekked his sauce spattered boots through the living room and hallway to reach his bedroom. He was a local kitchen worker feeding the entitled stomachs of the aristocratic citizens of his town. Though maybe not technically a peasant worker, as a farmhand might be considered, Cameron still occupied the lower end of the social status defined by his income and quality of living. A meager servant of the well-off, never batting an eyelash to perfect the preferences of the customers' taste.

This status of people Cameron could be categorized within, seem to take on a similar shape when wholly examined. Many of them fearful of authority, and if not fearful then disrespectful. Many saturated in alcohol, aiding to blind themselves from the struggles of their laborious, unending workweeks. Many with no more than a few dozen dusty, canned food goods in their pantry and half squeezed condiments in their iceboxes. Many having settled for a stagnant place in the job they work, giving up the hopes of a raise or promotion and waiting for the day that they can quit to find another job that will bring the same pattern of stillness. Many with empty or unreachable plans of a future, an undying feeling of potential to bring to the world if only given the proper pay, the proper opportunity, and the proper time to execute their inner ambitions. Many with five to seven years of lost time within their twenties, which they try to account for, but finally realize that they're place in life was just never figured out, never thought through, and never achieved only because it was never attempted, leading to a deadness around the inner iris of their eyes that screams, "I've lost it! I'd pay anything for a second go!" Many, also, with dumpster-dived furniture, dirty floors, and unpaid bills. Cameron, dear Reader, is just a single example of the thousands living in this town. The difference comes in the superficial details of his life.

Cameron Crumb was a gaunt, Anglo-Saxon romantic with seemingly too much drive for the amount of sadness and insecurity he held for himself. He was a long way from home, but seemingly so close to approaching one, waiting for that word, home, to strike a string at his core. His dark brown hair never seemed to keep clean, even after showers, and his kinked neck jutted from his shoulders like a palm tree. He sometimes had this to say to himself: "Every ravaged person was once a little child, and every horrendous flood was once a single raindrop." And sometimes he had this to say to himself: "I was going somewhere... just as they were." And sometimes this: "I'd rather sit festering in my self sorrow, loneliness, and aching than loose time in numb nothingness." But more times than not, it was along the lines of this: "What time is it?" or "I can't wait for a morning off tomorrow," or "I'm definitely getting a drink after work," or "how many days until rent is due again?" or "if I had a week off, I'd go to the mountains." He walked or bussed around town and, because of that, wore out shoe-soles quickly. He was entering his twenty-fourth winter and had four hundred dollars a week to show for it. He thought he identified with "The Road Not Taken" by Robert Frost, but most of his affinity was paralleled through his life's fantasies, not his true actions, and that has made all the difference.

What got on Cameron's nerves about his status in life, was the surface-level camaraderie that floated around his peers, but the inner arrogance that bubbled underneath. He wanted to believe that if only the disadvantaged came together, if only the more adverse individuals helped each others' weaknesses, a voice could be found to represent them and change the system of governing that kept them feeling so forgotten. But the poor, the people who have very little, hold pridefully to the things that they do have, opinions being their most abundant possession. Cameron had only ever gotten into arguments about how to change the country, despite how similar his opinions seemed to be to the person he was discussing with. Everyone was wrong and he was right. He was proud of what he had come to believe, even though deep down he knew that beliefs aren't to be proud of, but expected. Cameron, through this characteristic, was a hypocrite without ever being able to see his own hypocrisy. Sometimes those arguments would turn physical and it wasn't only one or two occasions that Cameron had awoke with a black eye, fat lip, bruised ribs, or bloody nose because of a drunken, escalating hostility between one proud peasant or another.

Upon arriving home, Cameron threw his knapsack to the foot of his unkempt bed, dug through his closet shelves for the small stack of money left from last week's paycheck, stuffed a couple twenties in his pocket, changed his soiled, white t-shirt, and turned around, to keep from losing his energetic nerve, to tromp back through the front door. The local bar sat in the heart of his neighborhood, like the spire in the St. Patrick's Cathedral, surrounded by the people of its community and as sacred to them as any cathedral was to the medieval Irish. Cameron pulled open the crooked, wooden front door and pushed through the disheveled, conversing patrons to the open stool three quarters down the bar. A heavy haze of cigarette smoke hung at the ceiling as the ventilation wasn't efficient enough to keep up with the chain smoking clientele. A bitter, draft beer was set down in front of him as he pulled out and packed his own cigarettes. The bartender knew what he liked. Now Reader, it is not merely being within such a familiar setting that inspires homeyness or relaxes the mind of these types of people, it is the steady pumping of keg after keg, the steady streams of urine flushing down the toilet, and the gradual drop into sleepy drunkenness that pulls at their satisfaction behind the walls of such a seedy, half-maintained establishment. Before a conversation could be had with Cameron, he must splash his thoughts in suds to lubricate the path from his brain to his mouth. The televisions flash spasmodically on the screen as he lets the colorful images reflect off his pupils, taking in nothing.

He was meeting someone, Kara again, and was trying to shake the butterflies from below his ribs. Even though they had been consistently seeing each other for around two months, Cameron couldn't keep himself from questioning his position in her life, as well as her position in his. And he remembered the other night.

It was mid evening, just before you can call it nighttime. He was thinking about what she had that he didn't have, thinking about what made her company worth enduring, what validated their time together. And she was thinking the same about him.

"I'm just taking it all in," she had said as they lounged, placid, under the ceiling and over the mattress. "You can't wear out you welcome when you make me so comfortable."

I like that, Cameron had thought.

"Where does it go?" she had asked an hour before, "where does that uncertainty toward passion root itself? I feel that everyone around me is on their way toward their own specific and important niche while I've lost part of my soul, or am slowly and continuously losing it. I'm becoming a person without an identity." The slow rain trickled down the screen on the other side of the window. Grey blanketed the sky. "I'm being chased away from myself."

"It only matters when you stop acting on your passions," he said. "That's when nothing has a chance. Even if nothing comes of it when someone tries, at least they tried. But to let it all pass is to truly fail." Her heartbeat bumped on his arm and her stomach gurgled. "That is to lose identity."

"It might change me," she said, looking down at her belly. "I might get scars that disfigure me from who I am now. I'm not against the ugliness, I accept it. But I will be different."

I like that, Cameron had thought.

"It's another perfect day to stay home from work," she had said the next morning, the grey blanket still engulfing the sky, still under the ceiling and over the mattress. "The sweeter parts of life really taste sweet when it all seems to be so bitter around."

I like that, Cameron had thought.

"Shut it off," she had said through unopened, drowsed eyelids, earlier that morning around the first light of dawn as his alarm repeated its buzzing cry while they both tried to sleep. "It's not time. Yaaawwn. It's not then." He stirred, spun, and slaked her wish. "We still have time."

I like that, Cameron had thought.

"I feel like it gives away too much," she had said about her face as he gazed at her the night before.

"It doesn't," he said, still studying, "I'm trying to decipher what you feel is so easily given away."

"You'll have to stay with me long enough to figure it out," she said after his confession.

I like that, Cameron had thought.

"I want to see you," she had said on the phone in the early evening just after the afternoon had deceased, before they had met up.

"I don't want to wear out my welcome," he said, worried that he might impose on her night. "I had a long day and I might not be good company."

"No one is good company, which is a tragedy," she said, "but everyone has something that you don't have and that always invalidates the tragedy."

I like that, Cameron had thought and the thought of that night while sitting at the bar gave him a small confidence, even though she often mentioned her close male friends and spoke redolently of her past relationships wallowing in the beauty of those people of her past as though she wished they could still be in her life. "I once dated a guy..." Kara would begin. "... and he was just so amazingly talented, such a wonderful and driven person," she would end. And she would be looking into the skylight or down the street as though that old reality were being displayed to her there. Cameron would feel that he was out of place in her life.

There were times when Cameron couldn't remember her last name, and when he finally decided on what it was, he felt the look of the word too ugly or unfitting for who she was. It was as if the man who passed it down to her had never really taught her how to use it and she left it in a drawer for years and years before realizing that it might be necessary to have in the big world, arbitrarily fiddling it into a working manner that she can troubleshoot to function, and then pull it out only when absolutely necessary. It wasn't hers and she knew it. He thought of the word in his mind in relation to her as he stared off on the barstool, letting the boisterousness of the other customers swirl around him. Too much talk of food; he was sick of hearing rambled line cooks discuss dishes. Too much talk of music; he was sick of hearing ratty, pawnshop-found musicians critique and play music from the jukebox. Too much talk of philosophy; he was sick of hearing self proclaimed scholars tinker with a grab bag of big ideas and ad-libbing them into a drunken discussion. "I know how to cook," he thought, "and I'm glad to be done with it for the day. I grasp music theory and I don't need these lost children trying to direct my taste. I have read theory and science and history and religion and I think what I think about it and I don't want to be told right and wrong by anyone." But he felt guilty for the inner hostility and took a deep breath. He knew that Zen isn't drinking a beer while theorizing about the world and the people around you, Zen was just drinking the beer.

Four beers were quickly drank between the time he entered the Irish pub and the time that Kara walked in. Cameron's belly was pressurized with the many nasal belches that beer brought him. Swallowed the small remnants of flat, golden liquid in his glass just as he felt a tickle flicker over the back of his neck into his hair, lodging warmly in the dirty tangles. He turned to see Kara's lovely smile and a sensation of allayed anxiety flushed him. They sat together and spoke directly to each other, both doing their best to ignore rants and raves of their neighbors, glass after glass of iced whiskey drained, butt after butt of unfiltered cigarettes smeared into the ashtray.

Cameron used to hold a practical, ultra-realistic view of possibilities and opportunities. He had let the limits of the reality surrounding him work their constraints upon his ability to fantasize about the future. Instead of looking at the Mojave desert and saying, "I want to road trip across the country and camp under the desert stars for a week," he would say, "if I can work the next two months without spending money on booze, pay my rent and bills on time, and find someone with a car, I might be able to take a couple days off work and go on a two day fishing trip the next town over." He thought of the process and when someone came to him with grand ideas of traveling to Japan when he knew they could barely get through a workweek without starving, he bombarded them with questions of how and when and threw the reality of their situation in their face without ever letting someone soak in the necessary delusions of dreams. It was somewhat out of jealousy that he felt the need to anchor people back to earth, jealousy that he wasn't able to develop those dreams without realizing how impossible they were to achieve, or if not impossible, how time-consuming it would be to save and plan and the waiting and sacrificing before an attempt at achieving was graspable. But lately, with Kara, he had been able to suspend his own disbelief and succumb to the joys of speaking childishly about unachievable fantasies. Cameron has found that just letting himself see the very tip of such an iceberg, his true wants in life were beginning to become revealed. He has seen that being practical blinds you from the purity of wants, blinds you from the innocent dreams of childhood that gave you the belief that anything was possible at anytime for anyone; the world can be at your fingertips. Kara and him talked like this. Where they would go, how they would live, what type of job they would find that would suit them just right. They talked like this and truly believed it would someday, somehow come to fruition if they willed it hard enough.

In the morning, when all that willing went by without action, and when tomorrow the same willing would wash by without direction, Cameron, dry-mouthed and overly drowsy, would wake in his perpetual state of lostness. He would look at where he was, not where he talked about being, and he would see that moving is always one step first. And on top of it, when he woke that next morning, with Kara's petite back fitted into his belly and chest, he woke atop a soggy sheet with soaked pants. And Kara was soaked, too and it smelled like stale liquor and ammonia. Cameron looked at the clock. Still early and he didn't work until the afternoon. He thought, first, to take care of the urine-soiled bed before returning to slumber, but his head was heavy and his eyes were sticky so he just put his head back down saying, "fuckit."

She was embarrassed, as you would expect, Reader, and apologized, red faced, a few hours later after she had awoke. Cameron wasn't disgusted. Rather, he felt a sense of security from the puddle; she felt comfortable enough around him to fully relax. And it was almost as if she was animally marking the area against invisible, future prospective mates or threats. He thought, there's nothing about her that disgusts me. He showered.

The upper lip and cartilage in Cameron's nose were both soar, the lip swollen too. He noticed in the mirror that his left eye had a yellowish bruise coating the eyelid and a small purple tail that dripped out of the corner of his eye, like an oily teardrop. It was from the hand of some other poor, desperate, neighborhood peasant. A girl, older than Cameron, who was too drunk to maneuver her bike across the flat street, who was too drunk to accept help with her predicament, and who was drunk enough to attack anyone who might cause her a bit of embarrassment. She had hit Cameron after insulting the other people surrounding her. She had continued to swing until the bartender pulled her away and made everyone leave. "What a cunt!" he exclaimed to Kara on the surprised and fast walk back to his house. "What is wrong with people?"

"She's just trying to prove something to herself," Kara responded. "She got a hold of my hair. Hair pullers are god-damned cowards." She patted lightly the tender area. "She's trying to prove something."

Looking in the mirror, Cameron couldn't remember if he instigated some of the blows that he received or if they all came at him because he was the closest target. "You misogynist scum!" she had yelled as she furiously swung away. "You woman hater!" Cameron couldn't remember using any sexist language toward her. That would have been a little out of character for him. Or at least not within the character that he viewed himself to hold. In reality, Reader, he did not use any derogatory language, but instead insulted her on a personal level for being ferociously hostile and insulting, the actions and words of an angry, stingy, selfish, and overly prideful peasant, the details of which are not our concern. Oh well. Off to work.

Work had been passing by him, washing over him or around him. The fury of a busy rush, the shouting of an angered chef, the hellish heat of the stovetop burners, convection ovens, gas grills, and heat lamps sweating the alcohol toxins out through his pores and armpits, all mash together into a tangled web of senseless, timeless emotion and movement that never seems to root itself but float in a constant tumble; no direction was up or down and no path right or wrong. And then he would leave not remembering if he had a productive, satisfying shift or if it was exhausting and stressful. He awoke from the shift as one flips through the channels on a television during a commercial break. The fat-cats feasting in the dining room, guzzling top-shelf brandies and spooning microscopic tastes of expensive caviare with dainty movements into their jiggly cheeks, laughing importantly and loud as to let everyone surrounding them know that they are having a truly gay time, adjusting and smoothing their name-brand, tailored suits and dresses as they talk about their exclusive clubs, their ivy-league children, and their important business deals chomping and chomping and slurping and tonguing course after course of handmade meals crafted painstakingly by Cameron and his coworkers for a small hourly wage, tense from stress and sore from dehydration. Cameron let it all pass by him, washing over or around him.

Just where does peace come from, Reader? Just how does one, simple, struggling man push through the never ending disappointment and apprehension of an unsettled world, an inconsistent, unpredictable world? From Cameron's position, just as the position of the thousands of similar citizens, many choices and many dreams look futile due to the limits set by a society governed by class, favoring the ones who were born closer to opportunities, who had never faced the reality of being unfit or unfunded or uninformed for betterment or simple change in life. Being the forgotten ones, a community of outcasts who function behind the scenes and stay out of the system, staying away from the world at large and its overbearing magnitude, being secretly afraid of death and surveillance and police and the president and pollution, being left with the repercussions of a careless generation of parents and grandparents, all becomes too much for a broke, struggling, alcoholic, dreamer to handle. It all sends those peasants a sense of origin-less guilt. Cameron suffers from the symptoms of this pre-constructed world. So does Kara, and the drunken madwomen who busted Cameron's lip, and Cameron's friend Ben. It's just a matter of how each one responds to the symptoms, and then, how each one treats them. But, Reader, those people are still looking for some graspable peace. They're still looking for a way to anchor themselves, always afraid for the reality that they never will.

Cameron met Ben after work.

"Does peace come from within," Cameron asked while rolling a piece of lint in his fingers, "like the Buddhists say?" The bar was dim and music played lightly from the jukebox in the corner. Pool balls smashed into each other sporadically. "Are time and space and life and death all contained within the self and not enveloping us from the outside world?" Cameron didn't necessarily expect an answer.

"That's like asking, 'which air is more important; the air inside a balloon or the air outside?'" Ben said through a bushy beard. "It's all still air. The answer depends only on whether you want to be on the inside of the balloon or the outside."

Cameron thought for a moment. The answer satisfied him somehow, but didn't chip away at the helpless feeling he held. "What happens when the balloon is popped?"

Ben looked at Cameron for a moment, taking in the words and the image of the question. He sipped his beer, licked the foam from his mustache, and said, "who says it ever will, or that it hasn't already?" He pulled a smoke from his coat pocket. "When's the last time you checked?"

Ben was purposefully not giving Cameron any finality. Cameron wasn't even sure what his question was anymore. Ben just lit up his cigarette and leaned forward onto his elbows, waiting for the paradox to pass Cameron's mind, waiting for him to accept the ambiguity as to center himself with the fact that no one had an answer to give anyone else.

"I need a new job," Cameron said after a minute, lighting up a smoke of his own. "I'm getting worn too thin. I'm becoming numb."

"You should never ignore discomfort. How long have you been feeling this way?"

"I can't tell," he thought, "I can't say. It just gradually became the way I felt about the job and about my life." He ordered another round.

"Sounds like maybe you've told yourself one thing for too long when another thing was happening right in front of you. Maybe you wanted to see a monkey when there was only a rabbit in the cage," Ben said, then excused himself for the bathroom.

The bartender walked over to Cameron. He held a bag of chips in his hand, unopened. "You want these?" he asked.

Cameron looked up with a questioning curiosity painted on his face.

"Guy left 'em about twenty minutes ago. Don't think he's comin' back."

"Yah, I'll take 'em," he finally said, gratefully. "Thanks." He opened the bag and snacked while Ben left the bathroom and sat back down.

"Lets play those guys a game," he said gesturing with an imperceptible twitch of his neck to the pool players. "You play amateur at first and I'll carry you."

Cameron knew the routine. They dropped their stack of quarters down and together ran through a type of street theatre that was so convincing and well rehearsed, the two-man audience ended up paying for a performance that they never even realized they sat through; four games later, Cameron and Ben walked to another bar with fifty dollars extra.

"I always wonder why," Cameron said as they walked to the next bar, "why we're supposed to love animals and forgive man. Love the world but accept humanity. It's as though we're set up from the beginning to find flaws within our own existence and that everything outside of us is beautiful and perfect and should be seen as such while whatever we are is not good enough to love or find beautiful. But I know none of it's perfect."

"You seem too antagonistic toward the intrinsic attitude we've developed," Ben said casually. "Humanity is just too complicated, too difficult for humans to understand and therefore can only be accepted, not loved. We admit to our misunderstandings of humanity, where as we egotistically claim understanding to the rest of our world. Animals are simple, so we say. Their simplicity and predictive nature should be loved because it stands as a constant, a marker. Humans can't be seen as constant because we can only judge humans with human eyes and a human brain. We can't accurately pick out the simplicities that way." Cameron knew the alcohol was pumping into Ben quite strongly now. He elaborates more on issues that he, soberly, would fit into a small package. "But I see you don't want to accept that position."

"No, no I don't," Cameron muttered, head down. "I don't feel free when humanity cannot be loved."

They walked into the next bar, both with a small dizziness, and both finding it difficult to talk about anything.

The abstractness of their thoughts wouldn't allow anything small. They ordered a round and sat in silence for a long moment.

You might be wondering, Reader, how it is that a full account of someone's life can be told when within that account the subjects reveal the inability to wholly understand the complexity of the human experience. You might be seeing the words and the context spread out in front of you and conclude that this account titled "Twenty First Century Peasant" is fundamentally contradictory. You, Reader, might say to yourself, or out loud, "humanity is being simplified within this story and is therefore becoming something that can be loved, even when it is said to be much too complicated. Who does the storyteller think he is?" And, Reader, I would have to agree with your sudden anger. I would have to agree to the fact that this story is composed in a way to reveal in simple terms the details of a peasant-like life within the twenty-first century world. I would have to agree that the eyes that I'm viewing from are those of a human, inherently unable to grasp and therefore love the complexities of all humanity. But remember, Reader, a peasant is a simple creature. And even though in this world, a peasant is infinitely more intricate than in any other previous time, a peasant is still confined to a much tighter limit, a lesser education, a longer workday, and a concentrated social group. The beliefs and habits of such a person are defined and refined through those limits. A peasant can be loved. The only question left in your mind, Reader, should be where this storyteller sits in the social hierarchy. With that information, you will be able to judge whether the analysis made is hypocritical or not; for one peasant cannot understand the complexities of another. Or, possibly a second question, Reader; is the storyteller a human at all? Or a higher being? I have created Cameron Crumb for you, Reader, so it seems that I am a god to a certain extent. Therefore, my analysis of this being loses its hypocrisy.

A dense line of people packed themselves along the bar. The voices of these people boomed. Their gestures flailed. Cameron and Ben observed the energy with a small repulsion. The atmospheric mood was antithetical to their own.

"Should we head somewhere else?" Ben said, leaning on his elbow. Atmosphere effected his ability to enjoy himself more so than it did Cameron.

"Yah," Cameron answered, "sure."

They ordered some canned beers to go, but as they walked out and the drunkenness became full in their heads, Cameron began to feel tired and antisocial. He looked over at Ben and saw that his eyes were droopy and glassed over. He drank his beer, felt that he had exhausted his ability to converse, and said, "actually, I might just head on back."

"Yah?" Ben answered. "Give yourself some time to think."

They parted at the street corner.

In the neighborhood again, Cameron walked in the middle of the trafficless street, kicked pebbles and spat out the metallic taste of the watery, canned beer in his hand. The soft wind blew the leaves and loosened acorns which fell and bounced off car hoods with tiny tings. His head was dull. He stuck mindlessly to his goal of stepping straight home. There was an old man who lounged on the stairs of his porch, always at irregular hours, always looking overly tired, and always happy to greet Cameron. He sat there now. Cameron held a relationship with this man almost solely based on cigarettes. Some afternoons or nights the man asking Cameron for one, and sometimes offered one to Cameron. It was almost a sign of contention if Cameron turned down the offer. And it was a distancing feeling of dishonesty if he didn't give one to the man.

"Goo-night," the man waved.

"How you doing?" Cameron returned.

"Ahrite. You wanna cigret, man?"

"Uh, alright," Cameron reluctantly accepted and walked over to the porch railing.

"They good, ahmose like tastin' chocolate," he said as he handed the pack down. "No filta. I remember back-in-the-day my uncle been given me cigahs. Ahways big cigahs an' I grew up smokin' 'em. But I' partial ta these nah." As Cameron slipped the last stick out of the pack and lit it in his lips, the man trailed off his story with some incoherent noises and gave a slurry salutation and slunk inside the screen door, disappearing. Cameron walked the last two blocks home and finished smoking that symbol of neighborly acquaintance on the porch before retiring into a dreamless slumber, greeted by a dirty bowl of dried rice, a half drank plastic cup of water, and two unpaid electric bills upon his balsa wood coffee table.

It might be assumed that we all sit at the equator between infinities; behind us lies an infinite past, and ahead an infinite future. At every moment we are bisecting infinity. At every moment we are no further from the beginning and no closer to the end. But we are understood to be moving, both spatially and chronologically. At every moment, dear Reader, a paradox defines everything about the reality that we believe to exist in. Where does that leave us when we feel important? It leaves us still hopelessly running to a goal never achievable. Where does it leave us when we feel unimportant? It leaves us at the only meaningful point to ever exist. How does a human react to their paradoxical, or contradictory, involvement with this assumed reality? It seems that they often ignore it, and it seems that when it isn't ignored it doesn't help establish us much credibility. If every person, peasant or aristocrat, exists in the most important point to ever exist, we all assume an equal share of this importance. It is only within the human's habit of segregation that an arbitrary hierarchy is formed. At some points, Cameron thinks he begins to understand such broad conclusions. At some points he even feels humbled in his lower social position. But at other points the broad conclusions become frustrating and unfocussed. At some points Apeirophobia ignites a hasty denial of being everlastingly at the equator. Is it worth wondering about, Reader? Is it worth becoming fearful of? Is it worth subscribing to religion over, Reader? Mystery or uncertainty will push men and women to fraught excuses and call them answers.

He awoke to the nimbostratus-sky, glowing from behind bleakly with grey, diffused sunlight. The memory that popped into his mind was that of a dream he had had when he was six years old. Young Cameron was sitting on the basement floor of his childhood home surrounded by action figures, building blocks, plastic guns, model cars, and sports balls. It was a mess any kid would luxuriate ecstatically around in. But there was no one around him to enjoy his riches with, and the stairs that normally led to the upstairs kitchen were bricked off. The windows at the top corners of the basement walls were black because the room young Cameron sat in existed within the empty vacuum of space. He longed for company. He longed and longed and longed until finally a parade of familiar neighborhood friends and family stomped out from the back room in single-file, all stark nude, and all, whether they were male or female, sporting erect penises. At the age of six, Cameron had never seen the genitals of a woman, therefore concluded that women had the same ornament as he did. He commenced to playing energetically around the basement and piggy-backing around on some of his friends. Whatever difference there was between the people he knew to be boys and the people he knew to be girls gave him complete opposite sexual reactions. He remembered waking from the dream atop his wooden bunk-bed, and feeling as though many curiosities of his young life had been satisfied; the biggest being the sight of a naked woman. Why this memory had flushed into Cameron's mind so many years later was a mystery to him. He also remembered, years later, that upon the sight of a woman's natural body, he was not shocked at the difference in genitals. It was as if he had always known his dreamed assumption to be wrong, as if he was using that image as a stand-in for when the time might come for the truth to write itself in. He lost no pride in finding out his idea of the world was wrong and he took no shame in changing his view of the world to reflect the reality, rather than denying and holding to misinformation on the sole purpose of appeasing an insecure ego. This humble characteristic had continued to follow him.

Cameron noticed his phone lying on the floor amidst a trail of discarded articles of clothing which lead from the bathroom to his bedside. The phone was lit up. It must have just rang. He opened it seeing a number of missed calls; Mother, Marco, Kara, Kyle, Ashley. He shut the phone and pulled on his pants. After brushing his teeth and guzzling a large glass of water to subside the dehydrated headache he carried inside his skull, Cameron fled from the low ceilinged house. He looked at the list of calls again on his phone and decided not to return any except Kara's. The thought of speaking to his mother was exhausting, even though he knew the conversation would be little more than a few words of salutation just to reassure her that he was alive and well. The other three numbers were of unknown reasons. If the importance of those calls rose above mere offers of coffee or lunch than the person would make another effort to get in contact with Cameron again soon, and then he would feel obligated to respond. But until or unless that happened, Cameron put their outreach out of mind.

"Hello?"

"Hey," she said back.

"Did you call?" he asked, knowing the answer.

"Ya," she said, "I was seeing if you wanted to get together before work today, but I'm already on my way."

"Oh," Cameron began, "I just woke up. My phone was on vibrate." His mind was in many different places at once as the sun forced him to squint his unadjusted eyes. He felt guilty as though he were lying to her, even though what he said was true.

There was an awkward pause, which heightened his feeling of guilt, before she faded in again, "...okay... well I'll let you get back to what you were doing. Let me know if you want to hang out soon..."

"I'm not doing anything important," he shot back in an attempt to settle the growing distance between them. "Uh, yah, but I'll let you work. Lets do something soon."

"Ya," she said, "I'd like that."

"Bye."

"Okay, bye." He felt as though they might not see each other for a while. The feeling dropped his stomach like a mourner drops flowers on a grave.

They both hung up. Cameron felt moronic and realized that he didn't know where he was heading or why. But the chain-linked fences, and the running boards tossed across the unfinished house foundations, and the dirty smell of traffic, and the long strings of sunlight strung like Christmas lights from every reflective surface, and the pitter patter footsteps moving in every which direction, and the scattered gravel spread sparsely across the sidewalk, screeching under his boots, kept his mind distracted. His backpack, stuffed with an unnecessary amount of crumpled papers and pamphlets and loose change, slung from his shoulders swayingly. A moist warmth tucked itself inside his pungent armpits. The wind kept reminding him of an old poem he recited in middle school of which he had forgotten the name. It was within these successions of instances a strolling man bumped Cameron's elbow, glared accusingly at him, and reminded Cameron that he was still a part of it all. He was still inside this place, with all of them, still subject to the law, taking up space like a dollar store doll on the neighbor's deadpan porch. He was not invisible from the scheme of things like Maupassant's Eiffel tower.

Cameron threw his cigarette butt in the wiggling weeds of the overgrown parkway and waited for the traffic light to flip as he exhaled the tail end of smoke from his lungs. As he walked across the four lane boulevard toward the crabapple tree he knew to be hidden behind the corner house, a childhood memory leapt to Cameron's imagination, somehow tied to the dream, or the running boards, or the poem. He pictured himself stuck inside the lamplit yellow of his childhood bedroom looking longingly out the window, like a princess cursed by a witch to a castle tower, at all the neighboring backyards as his peers played in the sandboxes and on the swing sets, joyously. Cameron was itchy and irritated, scabbed and bloody from a case of chickenpox. It was his second round of the illness. He felt cheated because he was told he would only go through the torture once in his life. But there he was, again, quarantined to his bedroom, pining for freedom. Maybe it was the crabapple tree that sparked the memory.

As Cameron scuffled passed the crabapple tree on the sidewalk, a distinct familiarity to the species churned his repressed nostalgias within. And with that lonesome, window watching memory of chickenpox came an array of other long forgotten happenings of himself as a preteen. Walking to school everyday in first grade, he and his brothers needed to follow a half mile of winding pond shore owned by a gang of nesting, territorial geese. With the geese's stature matching their own, their intimidation usually kicked them into a run at the first sign of threatening honks. The geese charge, mouth open and wings spread like slow, uncoordinated linebackers after the man carrying the ball, while Cameron's group worriedly fled for, what seemed to be, their lives. Every so often, one or two geese would attempt to take flight, but rather make a floating, anti-gravity hop toward them. Cameron became cornered during one of these episodes, water behind and to the right of him with an obtruded goose closing in ahead. Put into the position of defense, he found no option than to unhook his book bag from his shoulder while grasping one of the straps and blindingly swung it like a flail at the merciless beast. Upon the connection, he opened his eyes to see the mess of feathers blasted off the oil-green, mucky shore tumbling into the opaque, dark-cyan pond waters. Then, he sprinted desperately toward the brick schoolhouse. There was a crabapple tree in the yard across the street from his childhood home visible from his bedroom window, as well as from the goose pond. It stood quietly alone in the center of the yard, like a meditating monk, surrounded by the inedibly sour, worm-ridden fruits which dropped from its branches. The crabapple tree never made sense to Cameron. He'd tried to eat from it once, very young, and spat it instantly out into the grass.

Walking passed it on this day, as an adult, the plant still left him curious as to its functionless presence, like a piano in the house of a tone-deaf old widow who'd never read a line of music. The owners of the tree weren't hungry, nor were they offering their bountiful supply of distasteful fruit to guests. They just sat as the plant endlessly ripened apple after apple, watching them bud, grow, drop, and rot, attracting swarms of flies to feast, attracting mischievous children to throw at one another or at houses and cars.

He walked passed the tree, staring stupefied. When he turned his head back ahead of him, a woman and her stroller nearly swept out Cameron's legs, reminding him that he was still a part of it all. He was still inside this place, with all of them, still subject to the law, taking up space like a dollar store doll on the neighbor's deadpan porch. He was not invisible from the scheme of things, like Emily Dickinson's presence.

He turned the corner of the familiar neighborhood street toward the forever abandoned, graffiti covered complex jutting from the tree-scape a mile down the horizon. Cameron had heard a dozen gunshots from that direction last night. Perhaps they were only in his ephemeral dreamworld. Either way, the complex inspired a sense of insecurity within his stomach. In the neighborhoods, he walked down the center of the street avoiding the unkempt, narrow brick sidewalks, avoiding the feral cats glaring from within the blooming bushes shouting with their eyes to stay back, avoiding doorways and porches of the humble people living around him. He lit another cigarette and paused in the shade of the ramshackle First Baptist Church of Our Lord. The smoke had nowhere to travel but up as the windless afternoon hung above the city like a painter above his blank canvas, waiting, thinking. This day was open for inspiration, if one was susceptible to it. If one took a second to wonder why the time seemed to move when nothing else did, or why we can feel homogenous despite our separation, or why in one direction, time moves endlessly back and in the other it moves endlessly forward; the equator. It was all in this day.

Cameron jumped to the sound of a car horn blasting at him from behind as he scurried out from the middle of the road to let it pass, reminding him that he was still a part of it all. He was still inside this place, with all of them... "And I'm going somewhere... somewhere, just as they are," and just as you are, Reader...

AUTHOR BIOGRAPHIES

Jason Affolder

Once upon a time in the midwest, Jason Affolder was born on a freight train. After mastering the art of karaoke he began traveling the globe and making up stories. He fights fires in his spare time.

www.gargantuan-things.com
www.vimeo.com/jasonaffolder

X.C. Atkins

X.C. Atkins lives and writes in New Orleans. His work has appeared in Whole Beast Rag, Annalemma, Richmond Noir, and other journals and magazines. He also makes zines with his friends at Crummy House, based out of Austin, Texas.

Joe Barbara

Joe Barbara is a New Orleans native who has worked as a professional vocalist and guitarist for most of his life. He also worked as a clinical social worker. Joe started writing fiction after Hurricane Katrina. His first short story appeared in the anthology *Something in the Water: Louisiana Stories.* He has published haiku in *Frogpond Journal; A Hundred Gourds; and Acorn.* Joe is currently putting together a collection of his short stories, many of which are influenced by his life as a New Orleans musician.

Amy Conner

Amy Conner has lived in New Orleans for most of her life and currently resides in the Historic Treme neighborhood with her dogs, Baggage and Weasel, and a surly old pirate of a cat, Tarzan. From the first night of her arrival in the city, she has been a huge fan of the local bar scene. *Solstice* is her first published short story, but her novel, *The Right Thing,* will be published by Kensington Press in June of 2014. The website, amyconner.info, is promised to be up and running in the very near future.

P. Curran

P. Curran lives in the Ninth Ward and has written the novels NAUGHT BUT A SHADOW and THE BREATH-TAKING CHRISTA P as well as the collection STAY OUT OF NEW ORLEANS.

Rex Dingler

Michael "Rex" Dingler is a New Orleans artist, writer, and native who founded NoLA Rising, a public art campaign that encourages street art to positively interact with the community. Following Katrina, Rex began placing custom artwork around New Orleans in hopes of encouraging people positively in their return home. Since placing over three thousand custom signs across New Orleans, Rex has exhibited in New Orleans, New York, Los Angeles, Sonoma and Tel Aviv and had artwork on public display in over 30 countries. Rex is subject of debate on numerous websites in the States and abroad, most notably in the Village Voice and CultureBot, where he was deemed the founder of the largest grassroots movement in the contemporary art scene in the American South.

Rex has been published in numerous national and international publications and has work available on Amazon and Blurb, most notably, Rexism, which is a compilation of six self-published zines originally offered in anarchist bookstores across the U.S.

J. Michael Hinkhouse

There's no shape, no position, no structure, no relevant past, no planned future. I'm only here, now, looking like this, feeling like that, searching for something, but never finding it and always forgetting what it is and looks like. I'll wake up again and I'll run back through the land until I've exhausted my nerves and fried my mind. Look at me nicely and I'll live with love forever, look at me meanly and I'll hope for the best. I know you better than I know myself and I'd expect that you'll end up knowing me better than I know myself. We can meet, but not speak. We can laugh because we didn't speak. We can smile at each other and fill each other with love forever. I've got nothing to teach. I don't like telling people what to do or how to live. I've got everything to learn. I don't know anything about my surrounding world. I've got myself to share. I have a churning mind that will torture me till the day I die and what goes on within it is as much yours as it is mine. But it isn't a lesson. I don't believe in asking for forgiveness upon death, we should live as if we'll never be forgiven. Forget God, forget philosophy, forget politics. We're different. We think different. We speak different. We act different. But we will all die. And we are all living now. So let us also forget about death and focus only on what we are doing together; living.

Dave Holt

Prior to taking creative writing classes, my writing was mostly limited to song lyrics and poetry. My desire to write comes partly from my voracious love of reading and years of storytelling.

Leonard Lopp

Leonard Lopp is a photographer and documentarian. He has driven almost every street in the city of New Orleans behind the wheel of a licensed taxi cab. HACK is a year long documentation of a very unique year in the history of New Orleans when pigs actually flew.

www.leonardlopp.com

Jacquelyn Milan

Jacquelyn Milan is the author of several short stories, essays and articles set in New Orleans, her native city. Her writings have been published in *Big Muddy, The St. Petersburg Times* and *Louisiana Cultural Vistas.*

James Nolan

James Nolan's latest book is *Higher Ground*, a novel awarded a William Faulkner-Wisdom Gold Medal and the 2012 Independent Publishers Gold Medal in Southern Fiction. His *Perpetual Care: Stories* won the 2009 Next-Generation Indie Book Award for Best Short Story Collection. He has published five previous books of poetry, poetry in translation, and personal essays, and is a frequent contributor to *Boulevard.* A former writer-in-residence at both Tulane and Loyola universities, he presently teaches creative writing workshops at the Arts Council in his native New Orleans.

Carolyn Perry

Carolyn Perry taught English for many years at Lock Haven University in Pennsylvania. She now lives and writes in New Orleans. Her memoir *For Better, For Worse: Patient in the Maelstrom*, focusing on her experiences during and after Hurricane Katrina, is available from Sunbury Press (2011), and her writing appears in the anthology *New Orleans by New Orleans* (2012). Like so many who fall in love with the Crescent City, she's passionate about the people, history, and most special culture of her adopted city, and she's happy to join in this collective toast to New Orleans.

R.A.W.

Robert Alabama Wailer, aka RAW, does not like vegetables. He hates carrots, zucchini, and freshly cleaned mirrors. But most of all he hates onions. If he comes at you in a dark bar with a broken bottle, whip a handful of cooked onions in his face and watch as the scared little bastard runs screaming into the night, damning all the gods he doesn't believe in for giving birth to such a foul monstrosity. He grew up in Allentown, Penn., was educated in a whorehouse in Mississippi where Miss Penny Rose Toes taught him how to love but never be loved, and currently makes his living in New Orleans as a cigarette-scarred frog farmer. He is a fool and a blight on human existence.

9/24

Made in the USA
San Bernardino, CA
04 September 2017